DUMB BLONDE

Men want her. Women want to
be her friend. She'll enjoy all
of this until time runs out.

Heather Curlee Novak

Lazy Bombshell

ISBN-13: 9798992415100
ISBN-10: 1477123456

Cover design by: Get Covers and Heather Novak
Library of Congress Control Number: 2018675309
Printed in the United States of America

This book is for all the women in my life, past and present. You are glorious and precious to me. Your life against mine has created and guided me into who I am today. Thank you for your love, conflict, trials, late nights, early mornings, hard conversations and time. You are deeply loved in every timeline.

This book is dedicated to the Nerds, the Geeks, the Fat people, the Gamers, the Dreamers, the Quirky and the Misunderstood. You deserve to enjoy life just as you are, right in this moment. Please do not settle for anything but the best of everything.

"I don't mind being in a man's world as long as I can be a woman in it."

MARILYN MONROE

CONTENTS

CHAPTER 1

The Prince and the Showgirl

She wasn't alone or lonely. Life's lessons had landed squarely on her shoulders, and she was ready to live what she'd learned. She was not going to allow another greedy, dim-witted bottom feeder to take anything from her ever again. Natalie Zidler sauntered down the sidewalk of the quaint town, quite aware of the attention in her wake. The curvy woman swayed her full hips and tossed her lush blonde hair as she grinned at babies in strollers, assisted an older man with a shop door, and beamed at anyone making eye contact with her. She had a quick smile, toothy and generous like the rest of her. She was a sensational beauty, with her wide green eyes rimmed in thick lashes, a heart-shaped face, and full lips.

Some would consider her overweight, although her fleshy thighs and belly were easily overlooked when her large breasts and decollete were so enticing. She had given up trying to hide her body. She no longer apologized for who she was or for taking up space. Natalie dressed like a woman who loved herself, wrapping her generous curves in fabric that felt good and in styles that complimented her figure. She drew energy to her like a movie star, her shoulders back, chest out, moving through the world with confidence and an internal fire.

No man or woman would break her heart, take her money, or make her question herself ever again.

She completed paperwork on the home in Pepper Creek that morning, and now she needed a job to keep her busy. She walked into Pikk's Tavern and, after being greeted by the hostess, opted to sit at the bar. The place was cozy, dark, and quiet at four o'clock in the afternoon on a Wednesday. Smells of good food, rich people, and possibility filled her with anticipation.

"What'll it be?" The bartender grinned and looked uninteresting to her, like any big-city hottie in a tight black T-shirt. His dark hair was practically a crew cut, and his blue eyes were friendly and attentive to his customers.

"Can you make an Aviation?" She smiled with big eyes and open lips, watching for his response and secretly delighting in his hesitation.

"Uh, doesn't that have, err–"

She laughed coquettishly at him, expecting to change her order to make herself easier for the poor guy. "You know what? I'd really love a dirty martini with blue cheese olives if you have them?" She let her voice lift at the end, giving him all the control. Men loved that.

He loved that. He began nodding, mixing, and bustling behind the bar to make her cocktail.

She checked her new phone, and as expected, there were no messages.

The bartender let her know his name was Harold, and if she needed anything or was ready to order, he was her man.

She kept her smirk shuttered and just nodded at his helpful words. He was gay; she clocked that then. A future confidant, perhaps. The only other person at the bar was a frumpy older man who was attentive to his loud business phone call. She imagined he was the insecure type, needing to look important. She turned away from Frumpy and brought the chilled martini glass to her sparkling pink lips. The sharp flavors of vodka and spicy green olives, creamy blue cheese and brine flowed over her tongue, and she sighed with deep pleasure. Sure, she liked the uniqueness of the Aviation, but this dirty martini was her old favorite.

She looked around the restaurant, noting the smell of fried chicken, red meat, and the hint of sugary sweetness for later. Natalie turned to face the front windows, noticing it was quite bright outside. When she turned her head in the other direction, this place was all dark wood and secrets. Cool.

She faced Harold the bartender again, waved her fingers to grab his attention, and asked, "Are you hiring here?"

He looked at her a moment before replying. He wiped something on the bar between them, then studied her. "Not right now, but you know, turnover can happen." She nodded and sipped her martini.

"I'm new in town. Where would you suggest I look?" She opened her eyes wider and tipped her head. It was a move that looked only slightly helpless. She was aware of how pretty she looked when her wavy blonde hair tumbled over one shoulder. Her outfit today, a pink spandex top with a surplice neckline and stretchy black dress pants so comfortable she could wear them to a yoga class, was more innocent than usual. She watched Harold take her in again before responding. She admired him all the more for paying actual attention.

"I've heard Trailside needs good servers for the summer if that is what you are looking for. My friend Oliver works there." She felt a stir of hopefulness. He was serious. This was a good referral. She could tell he'd decided he liked her, and he'd given her a strong lead.

"Thank you, Harold." Her smile was real. She hoped somehow he would see that. "Oliver, that is who I should ask for?"

"Yup. Oliver Mutton. He's a good guy. You can trust him." He smiled at her, his blue eyes serious. He seemed to understand her and her fear, with all its false fronts and secrets, all at once and without a word. *How could he?* She'd barely said anything to him. Her heart leaped, and the blood in her veins sped up. A cool sweat broke out on her neck as she realized this man made her. He realized she had something going on where trust might matter. Their conversation was no longer casual. She thought she'd been casual and careful, but this man sensed her tension beyond her pretty smile. She kept the smile on her face but gathered her things to go.

She placed a twenty on the bar, leaned toward him, and said, "Thank you. Really. Thank you, Harold." He nodded and turned to ring out her check. When he turned back with her change, she was gone.

CHAPTER 2

Some Like it Hot

The place didn't feel like home yet. Her storage pods would arrive in a few days, and she needed more furniture. She'd purchased a queen-sized bed and a luxurious pink couch with down pillows. Natalie was living in the pool house of the big mansion she'd discovered in the Pepper Creek community for now. It was a small enough space that it didn't feel lonely the first few nights before she had her belongings delivered.

The pool house had a bedroom, full bath, living room, and galley kitchen along one wall. The bedroom had a window that faced the back garden, and the front of the pool house consisted of four sliding glass doors leading onto the patio surrounding the pool. Sheer curtains could slide across the glass doors, but it felt pretty exposed, facing the big house. Of course, the pool house was only meant for guests or all-day soirees poolside. It wasn't meant to be a full-time residence. She might need it to multitask for her.

The pool was a gorgeous kidney-shaped piece of art with teak furniture left behind by the previous owners. The garden beds around the pool area needed attention. It looked as if the groundskeeper might have been let go when they listed the house on Greenridge Circle. She'd need to call someone soon, or everything would just keel over and die.

Natalie poured a glass of lemonade into a paper cup and took in her surroundings. She still needed, or rather wanted, a job. Something to keep her occupied, a way to meet interesting people who wouldn't want more than a night's diversion. She hadn't left Chicago often to explore the surrounding world, and Valparaiso was still a mystery to her. She'd decided to move here because of Lake Michigan and the city being so close. The town was fun, like a miniature Chicago with nifty shops and fancy restaurants on every block. Central Park Plaza offered lots of action on the weekends, and Natalie already hoped to score tickets for the annual Winefest, Oktoberfest, and the like. The free concert series she read about from the Chamber of Commerce packet during the summer could be fun, too.

Natalie decided to have dinner at Trailside, scope it out, and see if this Oliver Mutton was working tonight. She rummaged through her boxes and suitcases to find the pink stretchy dress she loved. It might be too sexy for a job application, but with her body, everything clung and was too sexy. With her wide hips, large breasts, and tapered waist, she looked provocative even in basic jeans and a shirt. Unless she wore boxy old lady clothes in huge sizes, there was no mistaking her as all woman. Sure, she could stand to lose some weight, but she felt good. She was strong and exercised most days for at least a little bit. Yoga, cycling, and weightlifting all fired up her soul and made her feel like she could take on the world. With good lipstick and a pair of heels, of course. *Or a strapped young man underneath her.* Natalie sighed because that hadn't happened for a while now. She trailed her polished fingers along her own cheek, missing the touch from someone other than herself. She shifted to admire herself in the mirror.

She got the curves from her mama's side. Natalie remembered meals at her Grandma's red kitchen table; most of the farm food was decadent, with one exception. She found herself choking in disgust at the memory nightmare of tomato aspic salad. Just the thought of it made her throat close up in rebellion. Why in the absolute fuckery would a person add gelatin to tomato juice? Even worse, to place the horrifying, jiggly little terror onto a lettuce leaf and top it with mayonnaise, for God's sake! Her grandma made tasty meat and potatoes, served bread with everything, and that horrible, nasty aspic all the time. Her grandma would wheedle sweetly that jello would give her curves, bread would give her curves, and extra dessert would give her curves. Her grandma would know that since she had all kinds of curves.

As she dressed and applied her makeup, *Some Like It Hot* played on the fifty-inch TV the Best Buy guy talked her into buying. It dwarfed the rest of the room, but she felt Marilyn was almost life-sized this way. It felt like they were friends, sharing life. They had both been done dirty by fellas in their lives. They were both underestimated based on their sexy appearance. They both were alone in the world. Part of what appealed to Natalie about living in Indiana was the little-known fact that Marilyn's father, Otis, had lived in Indianapolis. Natalie found Indianapolis too sprawling for her. She'd liked the Carmel area, but Valparaiso felt right, far enough away from her old life to feel safe, interesting enough for her new life to be thrilling.

She perched on the edge of the bathroom counter in only a lacy pink bra and matching panties, her robe slung over her shoulders as she studied her reflection. One leg stretched to the floor to steady her precarious pose. Smiling at herself, she liked the slight sunburn that made her cheeks and nose glow without any bronzer. She swapped her usual baby pink lip color for a deeper mauve called Twig from Mac. She brushed her DIY lash extensions so they all lined up nicely when she fluttered them. She chose to add a black beauty mark on the right side above her lip. Dramatic? Yes! Why not? This was her season to do as she pleased without the weight of other people's expectations. She and Marilyn loved the beauty mark, and that was that.

Natalie gathered the essentials and stuffed them into a tiny bronze-colored purse before checking the window locks and letting herself out of the poolhouse. She followed the brick path around to the garage and slipped into her robin's egg blue Jeep. It smelled a little like McDonald's french fries, and as she pulled down the driveway and through the subdivision, she wondered if there was a gross random bag of food trash she'd overlooked. She liked to keep her car clean, but if some lone fry or greasy bag was hidden in the sneaky cracks, she'd root it out later.

She needed to fit in here, she considered as she drove past huge houses. She didn't want or need attention. Maybe she should find a different place to live. Maybe this fancy neighborhood was a bad choice. The manicured lawns and uppity neighbors could prove too interested in her as the new neighbor for her comfort level. Perhaps the pool house was a better fit for who she wanted to be.

As she followed the GPS toward the restaurant, she thought about Harold, the bartender again. He knew she was faking it, didn't he? But how? Unless he was all too familiar with hiding in plain sight, how could he possibly have made her like that? But, he did like her. She could tell by the way he looked at her that he saw through her facade and still approved of her. Harold's first impression was positive enough to refer her to his pal Oliver. Maybe she would go see him again. The pretty blonde shook her head at herself, her foolishness. *No. You aren't making any friends, remember?* She had planned to look after herself and keep everyone at a distance for their own safety and for her safety, too. She wouldn't be making any friends in Valparaiso. She couldn't take the risk.

CHAPTER 3

The Drip

Felix noticed her right away. He was clearing dirty plates from a table, sliding congealed food vehicles on top of each other, and marveling at the waste. So few people took home their leftovers. People seemed oblivious to the cost and care that went into their dining experience and just focused on themselves. He smiled at them, took their orders, cleared their dirty dishes, and took their money.

He lived well on the tips at Trailside. He often helped the other servers with their tables and sometimes covered their missed shifts completely. He was bored with the work, but he was invested in the success of the restaurant. And, of course, he loved Rose. He stayed mostly for her. She owned the Trailside, and unlike many eateries, her staff was well taken care of, so they were loyal. There was not a lot of turnover, and they had become like family in the three years Trailside had been open.

He carried the gross haul of dishes to the bus tub, watching the new arrival out of the corner of his eye. She was a knockout. Plumper than most would consider attractive, it looked like she'd been poured into her dress. The shape of her body was an ample hourglass, and her eyes sparkled with curiosity as he watched her survey the room.

She noticed him then, a look of surprise on her face when she realized she was being watched. She gave him a tentative smile before looking away. His mouth was suddenly dry, his guts twisted, and a lightness filled his chest. He felt like his brain had been filled to overflowing with champagne. Who was this woman?

He had to continue serving his tables, and it was getting busy. As he moved from table to kitchen to bar to bus tubs, he craned his neck to watch the blonde. The sexy woman talked to Kim, the hostess tonight, and then headed to the bar at the back of the restaurant. In between taking orders and wiping down tables, he saw she ordered something in a martini glass. It was pinkish, so he guessed it was their French Martini, with Absolut Vanilla, Chambord, Prosecco, and pineapple juice. A good choice for a girl, he supposed. She sat at the bar in her pink dress, drinking her pink drink. Waves of blonde hair were everywhere, and she looked like a famous person. Was she famous maybe?

"Dude!" Maisie's arm punch and one-word sentence rudely awakened Felix to reality. She was good at one-word communication, which somehow worked.

He laughed and mumbled, "Sorry! Um, what?"

His pink-haired coworker pointed to table four, who were engaged in conversation around their plates of food and drinks. "Brunette girl wants more soda." And with that, Maisie disappeared through the swinging kitchen doors.

He was thrilled about the soda, immediately making a beeline to the bar for the refill. He told Chip, the bartender, what he needed, then turned to the blonde. She kept her eyes on her cocktail, tracing the foot of the goblet with one dainty finger. He sighed, taking in the cleavage view while she wasn't looking at him.

"Man?" Chip held out the full glass. Felix was never as disappointed in Chip's speed as he was then. He'd hoped to catch the woman's attention, but he couldn't find the right words. She hadn't noticed him in the few seconds he stood there, and now he had the refill to deliver. He turned away from the bar and unhappily trudged away to give the brunette her drink.

He couldn't help but keep tabs on the blonde. He saw she ordered the tacos, switched to water after the martini, and talked to Chip throughout her meal. They laughed several times at whatever was said, and Felix decided he hated Chip. He couldn't compete, of course. He was almost six feet tall, which didn't seem to matter. His hair was a dull, boring brown and needed to be cut. He was slightly pudgy and didn't care about clothes. He wouldn't wear tight shirts when loose ones felt so good. He liked his old jeans and thought those tight ankle pants the slick GQ guys wore looked douchey. He'd stick with the wardrobe he had and be comfortable in his skin. Mostly.

Maybe he'd try going to the gym. He could stand to lose a few pounds and get a little healthier. Why did women always like the muscle-bound men? Couldn't they tell those guys only wanted one thing? *To admire themselves in a full-length mirror.* And the dudes were usually stupid, too? He didn't think Chip was stupid before, but if he kept laughing with her, Felix would change his mind.

The rest of his tables all needed him, and for the next half hour, he hustled hard for his dollar bills. He was so focused on trips to the kitchen and the front to cash out customers that he didn't see the blonde leave the restaurant. He clutched his order pad and stared at the bar, hoping she was just in the restroom. He realized after standing there stupidly for too long, she must have left while he was slammed. When he finally admitted she was gone, it felt like the sun set in his soul. He would do anything to see her again, even from a distance.

"See something you like, dude?" The caustic voice hit his ear right before Maise shoulder-checked him. He took a step, embarrassed and annoyed.

"Just watching my tables." He leaned against the wall, surveying the room.

Maisie laughed a high, tinny laugh and replied, "Sure. I saw you ogling those big ol' titties."

Felix felt protective anger swell in his chest. "Don't be like that, Maisie."

She rolled her eyes, then sobered, watching his face. "Oh, my Gawd. You are serious. You like her?" She gave him a light shoulder punch before they separated, attending to their customers, only to meet up again at the register a while later.

"You like her, huh?" Maisie was a good friend, but he couldn't find the words to fight her off tonight. In his silence, she kept going, "Did you talk to her? Did you get her number?"

"No." He collected change and headed to his table to finish their transaction.

Maisie joined him as he moved toward the kitchen again. "Why not? Felix, she was hot. I dunno if you have a shot, but you'll never –"

"Thank you, Hitch. I don't need a pep talk tonight." He heard Maisie scoff.

She elbowed him again from behind. "Good one, dude. Although that's not my favorite movie." She turned to the side to organize menus and salt and pepper shakers. She continued to talk as she worked. "I can see why you like it, though. You've also got that hopeless nerdy thing going on. You just aren't rich."

"What? No, I don't." He was offended, even though he knew deep down she was right. Maisie was probably as close to a best friend as Felix had. They had both started working together when

Trailside opened, and he liked the mouthy girl the minute he laid eyes on her. She was brash and almost rude, but you knew what she thought. She wasn't fake. While he tried to forget the moment, he had also asked her out. She turned him down, but having Maisie as a friend was way better than whatever else could have happened.

"You are totally whoever the nerd is in that movie. You know the portly accountant guy? You're kinda like that but without the money. Or body fat. Eat a cheeseburger, dude." She turned to study him and added, "And get some new clothes, maybe?" She handed him a bar rag to get him to help her. As they worked side by side, she continued, "I could take you shopping, you know. You could be like my own little Dude project."

"No, thank you," Felix said. "I'm just fine. I'm not here for a fashion show. I'm working." Felix hoped Maisie would get the hint, but she prattled on mercilessly. Where was the one-word Maisie? He missed that version of his friend.

"Yeah, but you get better tips when you look better. You're not awful-looking, but you could stand to go to the gym. And maybe get some clothes that are not from high school?" Maisie was probably right, but he wouldn't admit that to her.

As he looked her over, Felix realized she might actually be great at advising him on what to wear. She could be his own personal queer eye for the straight guy. Although, did that work with straight women? Or was she bisexual maybe?

What was she? Maisie was unique with her shock of hot pink hair and shaved sides. With the rock'n'roll hair, Felix would expect her to wear all black, but she usually wore florals. With her sharp mouth and one-word answers, she was a study of contrasts. She was a no-bullshit person, which he really liked. You always knew where you stood with her, and he thought she liked him. He thought that she would consider him a friend, too.

"You know what, Maisie, maybe I will let you help me in the wardrobe department." She grinned as she turned to him, eyes getting large. Before she began plodding and planning, he wanted to guide the budget. He asked, "What do you think? Target or Penny's?"

He heard a gagging sound and turned with alarm to see Maisie pretending to barf all over the menus they had just wiped down.

"What?" He asked, and she gave him a side-eye.

"I am happy to take you shopping, but I will not fucking go to Target or Penny's. What are we, our dads?"

"No, of course not. I was just kidding." He said weakly.

"Are you gonna buy me a little something?"

"We'll see if I live through the experience."

She laughed at this, and his face grew warm.

"Where, O great fashionista, would you take me shopping to make me more palatable to the world?"

DUMB BLONDE

Maisie dropped the bar cloth on the menus and tapped her chin with an index finger. Her nails were black. And shiny. With something scribbled on them. Felix didn't understand why anyone wanted black fingernails. "Marshalls or TJ Maxx usually have interesting things that maybe not everyone will have."

Felix nodded, feeling comfortable knowing that those places were inexpensive. Then he said, "Isn't there some kind of men's store downtown? I haven't been there, but I feel like I've seen the signs."

Maisie turned with fury in her eyes.

He quickly threw up his hands and began backing away, bumping into another server. "Oh, okay, I am so sorry," Felix muttered, both to the server and to Maisie. He scurried away from Maisie's mood to check on his tables. He was almost looking forward to shopping whenever they ended up going. He needed some help. It was time he accepted it.

CHAPTER 4

Singles Week

Natalie unpacked Target bags onto the small counter in the pool house. She put coffee, pasta, cans of soup, and Pop-Tarts in the cabinets. She put the full-size bottles of Dove shampoo and conditioner into the shower and put the tampons under the sink beside the new package of toilet paper. There wasn't a lot of storage space in the pool house since it wasn't meant to be lived in long term. She'd make do until she was ready for more. *You are being so weird about this.* She thought to herself. It wasn't that she was in hiding, but she wanted to keep a low profile. Laying low conflicted with her desire to have fun, let loose, and get some attention from the opposite sex. She'd been in a dry spell for almost six months, and she deserved some fun. She would just have to be smart about it.

Last night at Trailside, she'd enjoyed talking to the beefcake at the bar. She'd already forgotten his name, but she expected she'd learn it soon. She made arrangements to meet with the manager, Rose, later today. She couldn't justify using the bartender to end the dry spell when she planned to work with him. The only drawback of the night was the nerd who kept staring at her when he came to the bar for an order. She tried to avoid eye contact, but she took in the tall, brown-haired guy as socially awkward, at least, and a creeper at worst. He moved through the restaurant apologetically, afraid to take up space. Natalie knew the type. He probably lived in his mom's basement, played video games all night, and lived on coffee and citrus-scented vapes. Gross.

Natalie wanted to have some fun. She wanted to find a hunky fellow to take her to his bed, and then she'd go home to sleep in peace. She and the bartender kept a lively conversation with the other people eating at the bar. She'd asked him where to meet people since she was new in town. She asked him about himself, the restaurant, and the people who worked there. She'd even asked him about the nerdy guy creeping on her cleavage, and they laughed at his expense. The bartender assured her the guy was a good person; he just needed to get laid. She'd asked about Oliver, but he wasn't working. The bartender said Rose would be there at two the following day and that she should come in then.

With nothing but time to kill, the blonde slipped into a dark green vintage-style bathing suit and headed out to the pool. She had a novel to read and sun to catch. Natalie smoothed glittery bronzer onto her skin and considered her options. She could open up the usual dating apps and lose some control, or she could go out on the town and see who interested her. Of course, the kind of beasts she pursued tended to be at the gym, so maybe a gym membership was first. There are so many things to consider in a new town. She felt hopeful this would be the right place for her new start and she would be safe.

She lounged by the pool and fought the urge to Google him. She didn't know what she wanted the outcome to be. Images flittered into her mind when she slept and sometimes like this when she was still. She wouldn't make a mistake like that again, but she wanted to ensure the past didn't ruin her future. Natalie worried that Googling him might alert someone to her whereabouts. It is hard to tell what is true and what is fiction with Big Brother these days. She'd bought the Chicago paper a few times and didn't see anything compelling in the news. But then again, his people didn't operate in the light of day, so that probably didn't mean anything. They would cover it up.

She could reach out to the only other person who knew the situation, but they had agreed to part company. An agreement was an agreement. She'd left Chicago to get away from the situation. Why was it sticking in her head now? Natalie shivered in the warm sun and looked around nervously. The white privacy fence surrounded the entire pool area. There was a gate into the garden on either side of the house, but the entire pool house and pool were shrouded from prying eyes. She carefully eyed the back garden to reassure herself it was empty. Seeing the dried-out potted flowers and the browning grass, she remembered she'd need to call a gardening company ASAP. Natalie settled back against the lounge chair and closed her eyes. She felt like she was being watched, but that was ridiculous, right?

CHAPTER 5

The Job Interview

It was easy to get the interview at Trailside. She sat with the owner at a little table, her heart in her throat, when the worst interview question came out between them.

"So, Natalie, tell me about yourself?" The woman's voice reminded her of someone. The way the older woman drew out her vowels and spoke from the gut in that gravelly smoker's voice was a positive feeling, but she couldn't place it. Rose McCall owned the Trailside Bar and Restaurant. She looked like she was about seventy years old. Her face was heavily made up with red lips, thick black winged eyeliner, and too much rouge. She wore black drapey clothing and huge, colorful, chunky jewelry that looked expensive.

Despite her garish appearance, Natalie felt immediately at ease with the woman. She didn't even mind the directness of her first question. They sat together in a corner of the bar, Rose's back to the windows so she could see the entire restaurant at a glance. The beautiful wooded view out the window was distracting, especially because this was a job interview. Natalie cleared her throat and applied what she hoped looked like a warm smile.

"Well, I just moved here a few weeks ago from Chicago, where I've worked several places as a server and also filled in several types of jobs for the past ten years." She paused, watching Rose smile indulgently at her like a grandmother might.

"I'm sure you do well with your beauty, but we rely on skill here at Trailside. How do you handle the assholes?" Rose once again drew out the syllables, making the word *asshhh-holesss,* and it was all Natalie could do to keep a straight face.

"Well, my de-escalation skills are great. I've even had to take on the bouncer role when we got particularly busy, and several folks got rude or yelly. I'm not afraid of conflict." She had Rose's full attention and took a look around Trailside before adding, "I cannot imagine it gets rowdy here?" Her voice lifted up to invite Rose into confidence. The older woman nodded, her black bob swinging so neatly it had to be a wig.

"We are an upscale place in an upscale town. We do not require *(reee-choooiirrrr)* a bouncer. I will tell you, Dear, that Oliver put in a good word for you." Rose watched her, dark eyes shining. Natalie felt uncomfortable, as she hadn't met Oliver yet. Should she admit this? Obviously, Bartender Harold had been good to his word, but now she was in an awkward spot.

"That is so kind. I haven't been able to meet

him yet, but Oliver is the name of a friend who referred me here. First." *God, she sounded stupid.* Why was her education failing her? No matter. Rose was smiling wider now.

"Yes, Yes, I know. I'm glad to see you are honest – that is important to me." Both women eased against their chair backs then. There was a palpable shift in the interview. "Can you start as a server in a few days, assuming you are still interested?" Natalie beamed. It might be her first real smile in weeks.

"Yes! Thank you, Rose! Do you need to, uh, check my references or anything?" Natalie was worried about the background information she'd scribbled onto the application. She couldn't afford to have word getting back to her last employer, who was also his last employer. She'd kind of botched references and made up phone numbers, hoping a family-run place would hire her on her charm. "Because I actually left a bad situation. If you check references– " She choked up a bit.

Rose covered her hand in her wrinkled one, shaking her head, black bob swinging madly. "I am an excellent judge of character, and you are the perfect addition to Trailside." Her crinkly skin crumpled into a smile and then smoothed out as she stood up from the table.

Natalie stood, smoothing her black trousers and pulling her grey cardigan around her. She wanted to hug this woman she barely knew. She stood awkwardly and extended a hand, and they shook.

Rose pulled her into a half hug and said, "Welcome to the family, Natalie."

Natalie felt lighter and more at ease since leaving Chicago. She had a job at a good place, and she liked the owner immediately. Now, she needed to meet Oliver and thank him for the help. "Is Oliver here? I would like to meet him and thank him."

Rose shook her head and waved at someone behind them. "He comes in, in an hour, but Felix can show you around if you like?"

Natalie turned to face the nerd who stared too much from last night. He wore the same drab t-shirt and jeans from last night. She worked hard to keep a smile in place even as her stomach plunged. Would this creep stare at her during a tour, too? Could she beg off and avoid him?

Rose was taking them both by the arm to introduce them. "Natalie Zidler, this is Felix, our lead server. Felix, Natalie will be starting as a server shortly. Please show her around before she leaves, okay?" Rose's 'okay' came out *Ohhh-kaaayyyy* and almost felt endless.

Felix was the creeper's name, and he stood gobsmacked before her. He seemed to collect himself with a subtle nudge from Rose before she sashayed away. Natalie wondered if it was too late to quit this new job at Trailside, and then the guy opened his mouth.

"Hello there." He paused, trying to look

casual, she thought, and apparently struggling for words. "I saw you here last night, right? Welcome to Trailside!" Felix had a surprisingly beautiful voice that rumbled over her skin. He also had the good manners to not stare at her, instead turning to survey the room and decide where to start.

Maybe she didn't hate him. He had a loser vibe, but that wasn't her problem. She needed him to like her and to say nice things to Rose about her. She turned on her charm and said sweetly, "Thank you, Felix. I heard this was a good place to work. Oliver was supposed to be my contact, but I have yet to meet him. Does he actually work here?" They both laughed awkwardly.

Felix gestured she should follow him as he replied, "Yes, but not till dinner shift in an hour or so. He's a good guy."

She noticed annoyance across the boy's face even as he said the words. It made her more curious about this Oliver fellow. When they'd finished the impromptu training, Felix stood beside Natalie, and neither of them spoke. The kitchen doors swung open, and a streak of pink flew out carrying appetizers on a tray.

"Hey!" Maisie almost crashed into them but deftly rerouted and staggered towards a table of boisterous women laughing too much and too loudly. She delivered the food, and they watched from the safety of the wall beside the kitchen door.

"That is Maisie. Another thing to know is we never stand in front of the kitchen door." He laughed wryly.

Natalie replied, "Yeah, I got that." Felix chuckled, and Natalie thought his laugh sounded nice. He just needed to make an effort not to ogle women, and then he wouldn't be so creepy. Maisie looked fun to her. She grinned at them both as she headed back to them.

"So what is going on here, friends?" Maisie spoke fast and sounded amused. Natalie noticed Felix shot her a look.

"This is Natalie, a new server." Felix introduced the two women, and Maisie wiped her hands on her apron before taking Natalie's.

"Well, hello, Natalie, a New Server." Maisie winked at Felix and plunged through the swinging doors into the kitchen. They both laughed and turned to look out over the dining room.

"Well, I guess that's about it for now," Felix said.

Natalie could tell he wanted to keep her, but they could only go over so many things before she actually started a shift. She smiled at him warmly, in a way she knew should appear friendly but not inviting. Felix reminded her of a golden retriever puppy with the smile he gave back to her. Eager. Pleased to be praised and barking up the wrong tree.

They shook hands, and she took one step towards the door before noticing something exciting at the bar. Or someone. Having already dismissed Felix, she murmured under her breath, making Felix ask her to repeat the words.

"Oh! I said, 'I think I'm going to get a drink at the bar.'" She looked around to make sure Rose wasn't right there and headed toward the empty stool next to the tall tattooed fellow who had just come in. Felix said something she didn't hear.

"Why hello, what can I get for you?' A blonde female bartender greeted Natalie this time.

"Hi! I just started serving here and figured I'd have a little something before I headed home." The woman in bodycon black stood behind the bar and eyed her warily.

"Do you think that's a good idea?" Natalie laughed, covering her mouth and then grinning indulgently.

"Oh no, I mean, I'm not working right now. I won't start for a few days." The blonde laughed nervously and spread her arms wide.

"Well then, the bar is your limit! I'm Cheyenne. I only work weekends. When do you start?"

"In a few days. I was here the other night, and I had a really tasty little something in a champagne Coupe?"

"Oh yes, that's the French. Coming right up."

Natalie looked around to see who might be paying attention to what she's doing with her life. And sure enough, Felix is the only one whose eyes linger on hers. She gave him a dainty little finger wave and then turned to the big tattooed hunk to her right. There was no wedding ring; he was eating the tacos she enjoyed the other night, and it looked like he was drinking a Coke or something instead of a booze. She leaned slightly in his direction and used her sultry voice to initiate.

"Why, hello. What's a nice young man like you doing at a place like this?" The Hunk took a moment to turn to her, and she certainly hoped he realized she was making a joke. She didn't want a man who was too bright because they were boring and full of themselves. She liked a man who was just shy of dumb. Someone who would think the world hung on her toes but wouldn't try to mansplain the basics of life to her every single fucking day.

When the hunk finished turning to her, It took him several moments to raise his gaze from her cleavage to her eyes. Bingo! This guy was ripe for play.

"What? Don't knock Trailside." His voice didn't fit the exterior vision she was enjoying. It was higher than she'd expected, but she kept her face playful and interested.

"Oh, I'm so sorry, I was making a joke. Of course, it's a very nice place. Hey, I mean this in the best way, but you don't look like a very nice guy." His eyebrows raised for her to add something to the statement. "You look like the sort of trouble I'd like to get into tonight."

Natalie fluttered her lashes, looking away from him as if intimidated or nervous. She was neither of these things. This merely set the hook for her prey. Most men needed to feel in control, so she let them think they were. She knew how to take care of herself, and sometimes self-care meant taking a stranger home from the bar. The hunky stranger leaned towards her, wiping his mouth with a napkin and grinning.

"Oh, do I? What if I told you you looked like a little trouble that I would like to get into?"

She hoped her face didn't show that she hated his stupid joke. She wasn't here for conversation, so she couldn't let it derail her plans. She sipped at her drink, nursing it so she would still be safe to drive. While she felt fine picking up a guy at the place where she was going to be working, she had no intention of driving home inebriated. She might have been foolish from time to time, but she wasn't stupid or reckless like that.

She said nothing in reply but grinned wickedly at him. As they began to flirt more readily, Natalie was startled to have a napkin pushed against her elbow. She turned to see Maisie give her a wink as she picked up the folded napkin, discovering it was a note with **not Thor** scratched into the paper. Confused. She looked up to see Maisie and Felix standing side by side once again by the kitchen door, drawing their fingers across their throat in a kill motion.

Both shook their heads at her and laughed. She did a quick check to make sure the tattooed hunk wasn't catching all this, and as soon as she could discreetly excuse herself to the ladies' room, she went to figure out what all the fuss was about. She didn't even have to seek them out.

Maisie caught her right by the bathroom door. "I know that we don't know each other, but you do not want to bother with Thor."

"Is that really his name?"

"I don't know. I'm not sure what his name is. He's a regular. He's in here at least once a week, but he's as dumb as a box of rocks and takes home anyone willing."

Natalie hoped her inner delight did not show on her face. "Oh. Well. I don't usually look for smart guys in the first place." Natalie winked, and the two women shared in the joke. "I'm not looking for anything serious. We're just having a fun conversation."

Maisie gave her an appraising look, one eyebrow raised and the trademark smirk on her glossy lips. "Okay, but don't say I didn't warn you." She bounced off to take care of tables, and Natalie dipped into the restroom to check her face, touch up lipstick, and reapply perfume.

***

When she returned to the bar, The Hunk, AKA Thor, was paying their respective bills. She looked at her half-finished cocktail longingly and then up at him with what she knew would be an innocent and confused expression. He just grinned at her and traced her skin from her shoulder to her wrist. She shivered when his rough fingertips reached her bare arm.

"I thought maybe we would get out of here." Not a question. Her breath hitched, and her belly fluttered with anticipation. She wasn't going to have to work hard for this at all. Even without a low-cut dress, her charms were particular. She enjoyed the cat-and-mouse game of flirting. Natalie lived to asses and charm anyone she encountered, especially men. She smiled up at the tall man towering over her, looked down bashfully, and back up at him, meeting his icy blue eyes with hers. Flirting was her art form.

"Well, okay then. I usually don't accept dates from anonymous men." It was his turn to look surprised, and he chuckled.

"I'm Thomas," he said. "And you are the beautiful Natalie." She did not try to hide her surprise. He must have asked the bartender for her name, and she appreciated the effort. He put his hand against the small of her back to guide her through the restaurant. She might have blushed slightly when Maisie gave her a gagging motion behind his back. Felix was nowhere to be seen, and for some reason, she felt relief at this bit of luck.

In the parking lot, Natalie explained that she would follow him to his place. He offered his deck with a hot tub as their destination, and she laughed at his boldness. Of course, she agreed. He had her number, and she had his. Tonight was gonna be fun.

CHAPTER 6

Scudda Hoo! Scudda Hay!

As she drove her Jeep behind his car's tail lights, Natalie wasn't sure what to expect. She only knew his first name. Natalie felt a little bit sheepish about her wantonness tonight, but she knew that she had to keep people at a distance. Her impulses had landed her in hot water before...her last relationship was a painful example. She didn't want to have a boyfriend, just some stress release. A one-night stand would make her feel calmer and more confident going into her new work at Trailside. Thomas didn't seem like the kind of guy who would be a problem and maybe could become friends with benefits if he made it past the first stage tonight.

She parked in front of his house on a downtown street. She followed him as he headed up the front walk, and he reached back to take her hand and pull her to him.

"I'm really glad you talked to me at the bar tonight." His voice tickled over her ear, sending chills down her neck. It wasn't exactly Shakespeare, but again, she knew why she followed him here. A quick meal. There were benefits to the physical equivalent of a trashy diner meal. Sometimes, you just have to get a cheeseburger at the drive-through. She couldn't expect 4-star dining from a drive-through guy, so she lowered her expectations and smiled at his back. She followed him through the house, and he gestured to a 1970's bathroom.

"There are maybe swimsuits in there." He grinned wolfishly at her, and she fluttered her lashes. *How long do I have to wait to lock lips with this big guy?* As she shut the door between them and stripped out of her sensible work pants, she hummed tunelessly. The bathroom was dingy and so dated it made her teeth hurt. Brown tile, tub, and sink. *Yuck.* Natalie turned to the large frosted mirror to look at herself in the plum-colored lacy lingerie and decided it all needed to go.

Natalie took her time admiring herself. Her breasts were her favorite feature. They were full and large and fairly even. She had a little bit of a waist, even with the squishy belly and wide hips and thighs that expanded over the years. She raked her fingers through her curly pubes hoping he wasn't a guy who needed a bare pussy to go down on her. She worried about dudes who wanted some kind of little girl porno aesthetic.

No one knew her age, and Natalie certainly wasn't going to admit it to anyone. She knew she was a bigger girl, and she liked how she looked. She was soft and curvy and voluptuous. She looked like a person other people would want to cuddle, not like some skinny bitch who looked like they just were hungry all the time. Women were nasty to each other because they were always so hungry, so angry. Dessert kept people sweet. Cheeseburgers kept people huggable. She would never understand why a woman would starve themselves for any reason other than self-hatred. Women certainly should not do it to please a man. Real men liked real women.

Natalie had pleased several men, and her size wasn't normally found in the junior section. She shopped at Torrid and Lane Bryant, and more recently, she's been able to go with higher-end brands and more expensive clothing. It's been such a pleasure to buy clothes that felt good and were well made at prices she'd never imagined she'd be able to afford. Having money was delightful. Money gives a person choices and freedom.

She heard a patio door slide and some shuffling out where she thought the deck was. Natalie picked up the articles of clothing from the floor and folded them neatly as if she were at a doctor's office. Panties and bra in between shirt and pants. Why did people do that? Why did she hide her lingerie when she planned to walk out buck naked? Why still the very mindful, very demure choice to fold her undergarments inside her outer clothing? People were so weird, and she was *people*. She left her folded pile on the sink vanity, took a deep breath, and stepped out of the shagadelic bathroom.

The kitchen was still dim, the only light over the sink. His house smelled like cinnamon and apple, but not the good kind—like a Glade air freshener from the 1970's. It smelled plasticky and artificial, and she wondered if she would get a headache. She knew how to get rid of a headache.

Natalie could see twinkling light out through the sliding glass windows on the deck. A tall figure was moving around, removing a cover to the hot tub and lighting some candles. As he turned and saw her illuminated in the glow of the dim kitchen light, his jaw dropped open. She smiled at his reaction. Certainly, this Thomas guy gets a lot of action, looking like he does. Surely, he knew this was where this night was going. He moved quickly towards her, pausing only to open the sliding glass door, and stopped short before her. He said one word: "Wow."

"Like what you see?" She waited to make sure he knew what he was getting into, but he just stared and smiled, taking her all in. She felt her breasts tingle, and she pressed her thighs a little closer together as she enjoyed his ogling. She wore nothing but a smile.

He just nodded and gestured for her to join him out on the deck. Natalie sauntered past him, brushing her bare skin against his arm and reveling in the tease of it. He hurriedly shucked his swim trunks and followed her, penis bouncing comically. She got into the hot tub as gracefully as she could and stood, letting her skin get used to the hot water. Thomas also came to the hot tub and slid in across from her. They were both quiet, smiling at each other.

"So, Natalie, tell me all about you." His voice came out slow and formal. The beautiful naked woman in front of him just shook her head.

"No, thank you, Thomas. I'm pretty sure we both know we're not here to talk. Try again." She held her breath, wondering if he was going to be offended by her taking charge like this. He wasn't, he laughed and sunk down into the water. His body was only half covered and she could admire the ink across his pecs which were hairless. Was he a guy who liked no body hair on women too?

"Well..." He trailed off, uncertainty crossing his features, and it was all she could do not to laugh at him. She felt a little bored. She sank slowly down into the hot water, gasping as it hit the underside of her breasts and then covered them. The Jets created a vibration and noise that was distracting. She smiled at him again and slid to his side of the hot tub. As she turned her body to face him, her knee grazed his thigh, and he flinched. While she couldn't see under the water, she imagined she knew what made him flinch.

She put her elbow on the side of the hot tub and rested a hand against her face as she looked at him. She licked her lips once and then again before his eyes moved from her body to her face. He caught the second lip lick and looked at her.

He smelled good, chlorine and cologne. His breath was even minty, like he'd chewed gum in the car or popped a breath mint. She had done the same. He leaned toward her, going straight for her mouth, and she put her hand up against his chest to keep him from her.

"Oh no, Thomas. Don't be in such a hurry. We have all night." His eyes grew big, then narrowed.

"You said you didn't want to talk, so I thought–"

"Surely a good-looking man like yourself has a little more game than that. Just because I am naked in your hot tub doesn't mean I am a sure thing." She studied his face with amusement. For a moment, he looked like he would get mad, which would end things right then and there, but he decided to play along.

"You are just so fucking beautiful."

"I know," she purred against his ear.

He dipped his mouth to her throat and risked a kiss. And when she did not recoil or correct him, he continued kissing her throat. He trailed hot, wet, open kisses against her throat and up to her ear. He sucked her earlobe and the small gold earring she wore into his mouth. She could hear the metal clicking against his teeth, which gave her chills. Natalie shifted carefully towards him. His hands began exploring her arms again, and she could feel the calluses against her wet skin. He gently nibbled and scraped his teeth along her throat and shoulder, and Natalie's head fell backward. She lay back, exposed to his mouth. Her hands roamed his muscled chest, massaging his shoulders and pinching his nipples. Weirdly, he seemed to like it. She laughed to herself, once again confused as to why a pinched nipple did something for anyone. She was distracted from her thoughts when their mouths found each other.

He used too much damn tongue, and she recoiled immediately. She slapped her hand over his mouth. Denied, he looked annoyed until she moved over him, straddling him in the hot tub. She leaned toward his ear to whisper,

"I don't want to take all of your tongue at once. Woo me. Tease me. Take your time." She could feel him get hard against her body under the water. Without looking, she could tell this was an average-sized cock. She was disappointed with the huge, muscled size of this man that his package didn't match, but that would require less coaxing on her part. Not everyone wanted some huge dick the width of a Coke can. That shit would hurt!

Natalie was glad he didn't lose his erection at her correction. That was a good sign he aimed to please. She liked that in a man. He was an excellent student, in fact, and lipped and nibbled at her lips with his gently and slowly this time. Thomas kissed her lips, the side of her mouth, her nose! And then, finally, pressed his lips against hers, parting them before gently exploring her mouth with the tip of his tongue. Slowly, slowly, as

43

they breathed together, her lover sent more of his tongue into her mouth. After a while, she pulled away from him, smiling. She was delighted.

"Very good. I can tell you're an attentive lover; lucky me. Do you have condoms?"

"Yes," he gasped, touching himself under the water. "Do you want them now?"

"No, not yet; I just wanted to make sure that was part of the plan." She traced her damp fingers over his muscled arms. What did he do for a living, built like this? Maybe a desk job with lots of gym time? She studied his big, dumb face. He was so pretty. Thick lashes that were unfair on a dude. Tousled blonde hair that framed his cut features as he belonged on the cover of a Harlequin romance novel. He let her look him over, waiting. She almost giggled at how obedient a man could be when they wanted something, when they wanted her.

"Do you want to go inside?" She hadn't touched him down there yet. She'd only felt him hard against her belly when she straddled him. He was a little too eager, but she had been awfully bossy so far and had kept his interest, so she agreed.

"Sure..." They clambered awkwardly out of the water, and he handed her a large, soft bath sheet. It was too dark on the deck to see the color, but she felt the quality as she wrapped it around herself. He took her hand again, kissing her as they approached the patio door. He slid it open for her and then closed it behind them. He shot a glance back out on the deck, cursed under his breath, and went out to blow out the candles flickering around the hot tub.

"Never can be too careful," he explained when he returned. They kissed again, giggling and making out as they fumbled in the direction of his bedroom. Natalie got more of a picture of this hunk/Thor/Thomas fellow. He had fireman photos on his walls. As they made out against the counter, she glimpsed firetrucks on accent pieces in the kitchen. She finally stopped and pushed away from him to ask, "Wait, are you a firefighter?"

He laughed and caught her mouth in his. When he pulled back for a moment, he murmured, "Yes. You didn't know? Usually, that's what all the girls like."

Natalie turned and sashayed away from him, down the hall towards what she assumed would be his bedroom. Calling over her shoulder, she teased, "Darling, I am no girl."

He chased her through the hall and grabbed at her, cupping her ass in both his hands. He said, "I can see that. Clearly, you are all women." His hands groped along her hips and sighed, turning her to him. They once again locked lips, their sexual connection more fervent now.

The next doorway was his and opened into a king-size bed with a shiny, navy blue comforter and pillows. Natalie looked over the room as Thomas tugged at her towel. His teeth dragged over her shoulder, but she was dismayed at the story his bedroom told her. A nightstand was on one side, but no books were on it.

That was always a way she could tell what kind of person someone was. Did they have books on their nightstand, and what kind were they? Some might have fancier, popular titles upfront in their house on bookshelves for anyone to see, but what they really liked to read lived beside the bed. The lines they wanted to read late at night under the covers. These titles told her more about who they were. The books out front were who someone wanted to be, but the books in the bedroom were the true story.

He noticed she was taking in the room, and he stopped mauling her shoulder to ask, "Are you okay?"

She dragged her gaze back to his pretty face, kissing him with her full attention. She wasn't here for book club. She was here for uncomplicated stress relief. She practically tossed him onto his own bed, jolting the decorative pillows onto the floor.

He laughed, his towel flipping open. "Now, this is what I'm talking about!" A Cheshire cat grin filled his face, and he folded his arms behind his head. His erection bobbed almost comically as she stalked towards the bed.

Natalie released the fluffy grey towel around her, and it fell to the floor. She put one hand on her hip and traced her own collarbone with her other fingers, taking in his muscled physique. He was truly delicious. He began stroking his penis under her gaze. The dark blue of the bedding set off his tanned skin.

"Come here, you!" He reached for her, pulling her onto the bed with him, their bodies tumbling together, warm and cool from the evaporating water. He crushed her into him, running his hands all over her fleshy hips, full ass, and lower back. He squeezed and stroked her body, and their mouths fought a war everyone would win that night. She pushed him down against the pillows and ran her hands across his beautiful chest. Natalie began to lick and kiss her way from his shoulder down his chest, running her tongue over each nipple in turn. She nuzzled and nibbled and kissed his belly down to the frame of his hip bones. She fought the urge to bite the bone where it protruded. Instead, she grazed it with her teeth, and he gasped, his erection jumping again. It was distracting her with its humor.

Penises were so funny; such an awkward body part on a human. Both the tenderest of flesh and also the destroyer of women. Well, he was more of a conqueror, perhaps not quite a destroyer. She preferred men in a more reasonable range. She slowly began to kiss him from the hip bone to the base of his cock. Thomas grew very quiet and very still. She looked up at him, amusement in her eyes. She thought she saw a little spittle of drool fall from his lip.

"Am I making you drool?" She asks.

"What?" That was all he said. Obviously, all the blood in his body was right by her mouth and nowhere near his brain. That was quite fine with her tonight. He had his purpose and was fulfilling it so far.

She didn't even bother to answer, instead running her tongue up the side of his cock to the head and then stopping. She knew the air would cool the side of his penis, and he would be desperate for her mouth. She did it again on the other side, watching his face and then looking away. That was definitely drool. Kind of gross. Or was it hot? *No, I don't think so.* It was just gross. Natalie kept her eyes on his lovely bit of manhood instead. She closed her eyes and ran her tongue up around the head of his penis. The soft mushroom texture made her own body throb in anticipation. She held the head of his penis right outside her lips and heard him groan. He was well-behaved, and he wasn't insistent or bossy.

She breathed hot breath from her mouth over the head of him. And he grew quiet. She flicked her tongue out at the soft underneath of the frenulum before gently, slowly pressing it between her lips and into her mouth. She took her time with this part, sliding down his shaft as long and slow as she could. She wrapped her fingers around the base of it with one hand to keep herself from gagging. There was no need with him. His penis length was absolutely manageable. It was good to be in control.

His hands found her hair and fisted it as she moved her head up and down on him. She didn't know this man, but most could not last long during head, and she didn't like him enough yet to swallow. She also preferred to tease a lover until she got her orgasm, and a man satisfied was rarely motivated. She needed a motivated man tonight.

She slowly withdrew, and he whimpered, begging, "Baby, I..." She sat back, folding her legs underneath her and smiling patiently at him as he wriggled upright to pursue after her retreat. "Why did you stop?"

His gentle voice didn't sound mad, so she licked her lips and grinned. "I have worshipped you. Don't I get a turn?" She rounded her eyes and gave him a look she hoped was both come hither and still playful. He leaned towards her, splaying a hand over her belly, both pressing into the fat she used to be sensitive about and also pushing her back against the bed.

She wriggled to get her legs straightened, and he helped with a seductive grin of his own. The hand on her belly was caressing and squeezing her, his thumb grazing her belly button while the other hand stroked down the side of her body to her hip. He adjusted her body, pulling her to the edge of the bed along with the bunched bedding. Natalie lifted her head slightly to loosen her hair and saw him kneeling at the side of the bed between her knees. *Good boy.* She thought.

His method was more direct. His mouth engulfed her, and that bossy tongue of his was much better when applied to her lower region. His mouth on her made her clitoris tighten up, and he found the tight bud of her easily. Waves of pleasure and the newness of this stranger's body against hers were intoxicating. He stopped lapping at her before she came and moved over her easily. Natalie parted her legs as he slid the condom onto his penis. She often orgasmed quickly under her own expert hand, but with a partner, it could take longer. While Thomas wasn't the best lover she'd ever invited in, his eagerness set her into that luscious release ahead of schedule. Ripples of excruciating orgasm sent her voice into a joy-filled shriek that startled him into an orgasm of his own. They laughed together and pulled apart, panting in satisfied gasps. It was what she needed, at least.

"Thank you, Thomas. I think it was obvious that both of us needed this tonight." She fussed with her clothes and pulled out her car keys.

He pulled her closer again. "I think it was obvious to the neighbors, too." She laughed without even feigning embarrassment. She screamed because he made her body feel that good. No apologies should be offered for that. Or, maybe to the neighbors? He was still talking even as she turned away from him. "You sure you don't want to sleep here?"

She shook her head and continued to the front door. "No, you are sweet, but I like my own bed."

"Dang, Dude. You are like a guy!"

She turned back to him, absently caressing her own throat. "You didn't seem to find me mannish earlier."

Thomas grinned at her as he refilled his water glass from the sink. "Girl, you are all woman." He slurped some water and continued, "I just meant you know what you want; you leave after... most girls aren't like that."

She closed the distance between them, glaring at him suddenly. "Still with the 'girl' bullshit? Wasn't it clear you have just been with an actual grown-ass woman?"

Thomas threw his hands up, apologizing without a word.

"So maybe drop that from your vocabulary, Darling. It is dismissive and not at all sexy." She turned away without touching him again and walked out the front door.

CHAPTER 7

The Misfits

Restaurant work is a strange business, Natalie thought as she pretended to wipe clean menus to pass the time. Rose liked the staff to be busy, or as she said it, "ProooDUCTtive," in that weird way she had of over-pronouncing syllables. Natalie had worked at Trailside for a month now, but she still couldn't place the vocal affectation.

She kept her head down, learned the clientele, and chose who she liked to chat with on the staff, and who she did not. Servers Maisie and Felix, Mixologist Jessica, and, of course, the owner, Rose, made Natalie feel relaxed and made her laugh. She avoided Bartender Chip, who leered at her, and the busboys she secretly called Fric and Frac, who made whispered comments despite her intentional oversharing of daily tips.

Natalie liked the chatty Felix fellow despite his attempts to date her. He was not her type. Couldn't he see that? He asked her formally at first. That happened at the end of her first full week. They were closing up, and Rose insisted everyone had some kind of escort through the parking lot.

"So, Natalie, could I take you to dinner this week?"

She knew it was coming; his nervous body language was obvious. *The poor thing.* She enjoyed chatting with him at work, but he was both scrawny and pudgy simultaneously, so there was no physical attraction. "No, but thank you so much, Felix. You are so kind!"

He looked as if he'd expected the rejection, almost nodding along in agreement. He wished her a good night that got cut off as she closed her Jeep door with a thunk.

The next time was a few days later. They had a raucous conversation about a crazy table they'd had earlier that night. The conversation was between Maisie, Felix, a new guy, and herself. They all made up pretend lines for each of the customers; then, when they ran out of fun there, they made up ridiculous occupations for them.

Felix's comedic bits were the best, and he seemed to be a well-read man. She knew he volunteered with a men's shelter and thought highly of him for that. His comedic timing and thoughtfulness as a coworker were also good things. She just wasn't attracted to him, aside from his voice. She loved that voice of his. It was gravelly and hushed, as if every word he spoke was a secret for her. She felt attuned to his voice, as something sexy could maybe happen if she kept her eyes closed, and he just kept talking.

The laughter made her feel warm towards

all of them, and she wished she could invite the work friends over to her place. They might like the pool, but she really wanted to keep them separate from her real life for her safety and theirs. She and Felix stood side by side, and he just whispered to her in his gravelly voice, "Let's go to dinner later."

She smiled at him, admiring his persistence. It wasn't threatening like some men. He was sweet. She got the feeling he knew damn well she was out of his league, but he liked himself enough to pursue her anyway. "Aw gee, Felix. I have plans already." She smiled at him, pushed off the counter behind them and went to gather her belongings to leave. He slouched as he walked her out, chatting about the schedule, then staff gossip as she got into her jeep and drove home alone.

It wasn't the last time he tried. He was a persistent little fucker. "Hey Nat, we are all going to see a movie after work, wanna come?"

She stopped refilling the salad dressing and turned to face him. "Who?" He looked startled to be in this conversation and stuttered a bit before she continued, "Felix, we are friends. You are not my type. I do not want to kiss you or fuck you, okay?"

He stood there, slack-jawed and hurt. She felt almost guilty, but she wanted to be crystal clear. She liked this job, she liked him, and she wanted to protect her situation at Trailside. She patted his arm and asked, "Okay? Got it? I want you as a friend, not anything else."

He nodded then, cheered at the fact she wanted anything from him. Things were weird between them for a few days, but lately, he'd been normal, and Natalie felt relief.

***

"Why don't you guys come over after work tonight?" Natalie's voice felt strained, but nobody seemed to notice. Felix was mopping the main dining room, and Jessica was cleaning up the bar area. The rest of them had almost finished setting the chairs back down in the dining room and getting the setups ready for the next day.

Natalie knew she shouldn't have people over, but she had been feeling so lonely at the house. She spent most nights in the pool house because the smaller space felt warmer and cozier to her soul. A few times when she was exploring her new town, she felt like someone was watching her. Were they? When she turned to look furtively over her shoulder, there was never a menacing face in the crowd. *Stop it, Nat. You're getting so paranoid.*

Was he alive?

No.

With all that blood, he couldn't be.

She had decided to invite all her Trailside friends as long as Maisie could come. She wanted to be certain it would be a group, not just Felix. Her invitation came at the end of the night when she'd already checked with Maisie. Natalie knew she had snacks and drinks from a Target run earlier that day for a party. When she asked, they all nodded, and it was settled. There was going to be a little party at her place. The end of the night was a rough time for all of them. Having a tiny shindig to look forward to putting pep in their step. It was exhausting serving people.

***

After closing, Natalie drove slowly to Pepper Creek to make sure the convoy of the Trailside family was able to follow. She pulled into the driveway and parked in the garage of the huge, sprawling home. By the time she left the garage and stood on the driveway waiting for the others, they had all arrived and began coming up the driveway. All three gaped at the big house as they walked towards her.

"Uh, holy cow, this is your place?" asked Felix.

"What the fuck, Heiress!" was Maisie's response.

"Dude. This is awesome! " came from Jessica, who trailed behind the others.

Natalie had prepared for this mentally, so she looked embarrassed and shrugged.

"I actually live in the back, in the pool house." She watched everyone comprehend this new reality and take a little more time to stare up at the gorgeous two-story stone structure with huge glass windows.

The beautiful blonde gestured to the pool gate, lifting the heavy latch with a clunk and pushing the heavy privacy gate open to lead them through. They were murmuring quietly at the curving garden path that opened into the main pool area. They gasped again at the beautiful kidney-shaped pool sparkling under low lighting. Maisie plopped onto a wooden chaise and folded her arms behind her head.

"Well, this sucks. Too bad it isn't warm enough for a swim!" Natalie laughed, and Felix mimed shucking his pants and diving in. Natalie ushered them all into the pool house, giving a quick look around to make sure she hadn't left anything embarrassing out.

"Oh, this is cool, too," Felix said. Natalie gave him an indulgent smile as if she appreciated his encouragement. Her work friends ooh'd and ah'd over the colorful touches she had put in the pool house as they explored the small space.

Jessica noticed the aloe plant on the kitchen bar was wilting. "Do you mind if I water this?" she asked.

Natalie laughed, nodding. While Jessica took care of the dying plant, Natalie pulled short hobnail glasses in a rainbow of colors from the cabinet. "What can I get you all? I have Guinness, Rolling Rock, Stella Rosa...it's a sweet, bubbly wine, or I have the hard stuff.

"I would love a Guinness," Felix spoke up, "but does it have to go in that little glass?" His voice rumbled over her shoulder as he stood beside her. Natalie laughed and reached into the cabinet for a proper beer pint glass.

"What, you don't keep these in the freezer?" he asked with a grin on his face. Maisie smacked him on the back of the head and then reached across for the bottle of Stella Rosa. She poured it into a pink glass, holding it up to the light as it sparkled.

"Nat, these are gorgeous. I love these glasses; where are they from?" Natalie smiled with pleasure from Maisie's praise.

"Maybe Crate & Barrel? I really don't remember." Her friends began to help themselves from her assorted offerings, and Natalie dumped a bowl of sour cream and onion Krunchers potato chips into a red pottery bowl.

Felix stared at the bowl, and at one point rolled it to the side, keeping the chips from tumbling out to look at the bottom. "This is beautiful. I didn't think it came from a store."

Natalie bit her lip as she tried to remember where it came from. Probably an art show? She decided not to even answer him. When not working, she had been doing a lot of retail therapy to feather her new nest.

"What is it like to have the landlords across the pool?" was Maisie's next question, and Natalie demurred that they were nice enough. They didn't bother with her at all.

The four of them sat together on the floor,

even though there would have been enough room for them on the sectional in the corner. Natalie lit a few candles, and conversation rocketed between work gossip, Felix's new clothes credited to shopping with Maisie, and whether Natalie's breasts were real or enhanced.

As they chatted, Natalie learned that Felix was well traveled and this surprised her. He'd always seemed like such a shy person, but maybe it was just how he was when around her. She started to tune out the witty banter between the other three. She studied Felix's face, considering what she originally thought was insecurity was possibly just nerves because he liked her. That was a funny thought.

She normally didn't bother with someone who cared too much about her. She'd made that mistake of the past and wasn't going to again. If someone really cared enough to be nervous around her, then that was a novelty. He seemed confident talking with his friends, and she noticed that his knowledge of things was eclectic.

"I guess you could say I'm a jack of all trades and master of none," Felix quipped.

Maisie butted in and said, "You are shorting yourself. Felix, I don't know any other servers who have two degrees."

Jessica slapped him on the arm after hearing Maisie's comment, "You have two degrees?" Jessica repeated, "What the fuck are you doing serving at Trailside?"

Natalie realized she was flirting with him a little bit. She hadn't given Felix enough attention to notice before, but it seemed like Jessica was interested, and he was oblivious.

"Well, it's a good gig if you can get it. Not everyone is looking for a Bachelor of Arts in English and a Bachelor of Science in Psychology. Besides, there's a lot to do with psychology in the service industry." The three women stared at him until he confessed, "And I make good tips."

Jessica piped up, "The tips we make aren't that good."

Felix just shrugged with his sly grin, staying put.

"Couldn't you try to be a big CEO or maybe a shrink?" Maisie asked.

Felix sighed and said, "Now you sound like my mother, and as I told her, I would need an advanced degree to start some kind of therapy practice."

Everyone laughed as if they all knew his mother, and Natalie wondered to herself how close the three of them actually were. Felix assured them that someday he would grow up and get a big boy job.

He turned to Natalie as if he just realized she was there. His eyes widened as she smiled at him, a genuine girl next door smile. It was a rare smile without any artifice behind it. In the brief eye contact, she knew he recognized this. Felix should be appreciated, she thought to herself. He is good at his job and a smart guy. Natalie broke the connections between them and hopped up from the floor to refill her drink. Felix suddenly fell silent, and the conversation went on without him.

Both Jessica and Maisie made several attempts to dig into Natalie's backstory, but she would laugh it off and pour more drinks. Jessica's eyes grew heavy, and Natalie looked at the clock on the microwave to see that it was almost 2:30 am.

"If you guys want to crash, you're welcome to the couch. It pulls out or..." she trailed off, and everyone's focus turned to Jessica. She had sunk back against the pillows and begun to snore sweetly. The three laughed quietly. Maisie had only one or two glasses, and Natalie chuckled when she saw that Felix was still nursing the first Guinness from hours ago.

"No, thank you. That's so kind, but I'd rather sleep in my childhood room in my father's house like a codependent loser." Maisie said, laughing. She stood up and gathered her and Jessica's glasses to put on the counter. Felix looked around him, considering his options before Maisie sternly said, "Come on, Felix, you can walk me to my car. We'll let Jessica have a sleepover." Natalie smiled behind her hand as she saw Felix's crestfallen face. He looked like he didn't want to be walking out but wasn't hopeful enough to linger.

Maisie and her escort exited back out through the pool gate. Natalie moved to cover Jessica with a fuzzy blanket on the floor and tucked herself into her own bed. Natalie dropped off to sleep quickly, only to be awakened by an unsettling dream. She had been running through her neighborhood streets being pursued by someone, and when they finally closed in on her, she tripped and fell. The person chasing her caught her, but she could not see the face of her pursuer.

She woke up anxious and uncomfortable. She crept quietly out of bed to get some more water and check on Jessica, who had moved herself to the couch sometime during the night. She smiled at her tiny home in the dark. It was really nice to have friends over and to have made any friends at all. Her space had more life now, with the memories of the night, the conversations, the closeness of their little friend foursome. Rose was right when she said Trailside was like family. Natalie started to feel right at home in her new life.

CHAPTER 8

I Wanna Be Loved By You

She invited me over! Felix thought to himself. She actually invited me over to her house! Felix was buzzing as he gathered his sweatshirt from the locker in the break room. Suddenly, his knees gave out. Maisie was behind him, hitting the back of his knees with hers to make him fall back against her.

"Hey dude, you gonna score tonight?" She mocked him and gave him a teasing grin, adding, "The blonde finally invited you over."

He shook his head and said, "That blonde invited all of us. Natalie invited all of us, not just me."

"Yeah, but none of us are gonna make it. I can tell you're excited. Practically got a boner right then and there."

"Shut up, Maisie."

"Shut up, Maisie," she mimicked. "I'm just kidding. Aren't you glad you wore that shirt, though?" She nodded towards the black Henley he was wearing from their shopping adventure a few weeks ago. She looked serious for a moment, her hand on each of his shoulders. "Friend, just be yourself. If she doesn't go for you, then fuck her."

Maisie rolled her eyes, shook her head, and continued, "Well. I mean, on second thought: If she goes for you, then you get to fuck her, but not otherwise." Her usually confident voice trailed off, and he rolled his eyes at the pink-haired woman in front of him. She chortled and continued, "Oh, come on. You've had the hots for her since the moment she arrived at Trailside."

Felix nodded as he closed his locker and hoisted his bag. "You're right, but it's more than that. How many girls have come in here that I've tried to ask out?"

Maisie pretended to think and then looked at him with a "What?" look on her face. "All of them?" She tried to look serious but broke, laughing.

"Okay, okay. I didn't mean that. That's not a fair question." Felix admitted. Then continued, "How many have I actually been really into?"

Maisie's face grew serious, her eyebrow raised as the smile left her face. "Yeah, you've got a point. This is the first one, so don't fuck it up." Maisie sashayed out of the break room, and Felix followed behind her.

He looked forward to seeing the colorful inner sanctum of Natalie Zidler again and having her all to himself tonight. Unfortunately, when he entered the dining area, he saw the object of his affection in a heady conversation with that big neanderthal, Thor. They giggled at the bar and Felix watched in utter dismay as the big muscle-bound dumbass cupped Natalie's ass in one of his meaty paws. Felix stood dumbstruck and horrified, watching them until one of the kitchen staff elbowed him as they hustled past.

Thor took Natalie's hand and dragged her from the bar towards the front door. Felix stepped forward, uncertain but determined.

"Hey Nat?" His voice sounded strong... enough. "Are we still hanging out at your place?" She turned to him, lipstick still intact, a miracle, considering the kissing he'd just witnessed. Her emerald green eyes turned from lusty to sheepish.

"Oh...yeah, umm, no one could come tonight," Thor whispered something gross in her ear, and she blushed, stifling a giggle. "Another time, okay?" Felix watched them leave, utterly deflated. He was planning to come over. Was he 'nobody'? With a sigh he walked slowly to his car and headed back to his mom's house.

Yeah, Dude. You live with your mom. You are a nobody.

CHAPTER 9

River of No Return

The dining room lights were lowered just in time for the dinner crowd, and Rose bustled with the best of them, even at her undisclosed older age. It was the usual chaos at her beloved Trailside, and she smiled to herself, watching her kids and the staff run through their paces.

Rose, always at the center of the madness, was usually the loudest voice in the room. Her vulgar sense of humor, sharp wit, and no-nonsense attitude made her a force to be reckoned with. She was the one who cracked jokes that had everyone gasping for air, the one who kept the team's spirits high even on the worst days. She was the kind of woman who wore her confidence-like armor, deflecting anything that threatened her image with a well-timed quip or a sassy retort.

But today, something was wrong. Rose sat down heavily behind the hostess stand, her pale fingers trembling, the once vibrant red of her lipstick fading from her lips. She had felt it earlier — tightness in her chest, a strange pressure that she could chalk up to stress or maybe even anxiety.

As the morning dragged on, the pressure grew unbearable, and she found herself gasping for breath, feeling as though someone had shoved a heavy weight onto her chest. Was this it? Was it a heart attack?

She tried to push it aside. *It was nothing, right?* Just a bad day. Maybe the afternoon coffee was a bad idea. Maybe she just needed a moment to catch her breath. But now, the air felt thick and suffocating. Her pulse raced. Panic started to rise, but she wasn't about to let anyone see her like this. She didn't need help. She didn't need anyone fussing over her.

Rose glanced around the restaurant. No one was paying attention. Good. She could handle this on her own. But that's when dear, sweet Natalie appeared at her side.

Natalie was a great hire, and over the past few months, she'd become a favorite with staff and customers alike. She was curvy and had gorgeous green eyes that twinkled mischievously. Rose noticed Natalie flirting wildly with any male guests with muscles or tattoos. Rose understood, she too was a sucker for a bad boy. Unfortunately, she had also noticed Felix pining after Natalie like a lost soul. She should probably talk to him about it. She tried to give him space to live his own life. She needed Felix to be happy at Trailside, especially if her health was going to be a problem.

"Hey, Rose, you alright?" Natalie asked, raising an eyebrow as she crouched down beside her boss. Her tone was casual, but there was a hint of concern in her voice that Rose knew all too well.

Rose's heart thudded in her chest, and for a moment, she felt a rush of heat flood her face. She wanted to snap back with something sarcastic and tell Natalie to mind her own business, but instead, all she could do was force a weak smile. "Yes, I'm fine. Just, uh... just a little tired," she said. Her voice still had dramatic over pronunciation, but it came out hoarse. She immediately regretted the lie. Natalie wasn't buying it. She studied Rose closely, her sharp eyes narrowing.

"Rose, your face is all red. And you're breathing like you've run a marathon. You are not okay!"

Rose leaned back on the chair, trying to look nonchalant. Her hands were clammy, but she clenched them into fists to hide the trembling. She caressed tonight's red curly wig back from her face. "I said I'm fine, Natalie. Don't make a big deal out of it, okay? I'm just... having one of those days."

Natalie didn't move. She stayed right where she was, watching Rose with growing concern. "Okay, but I'm not stupid. You're not just 'having one of those days.' What's really going on?"

Rose opened her mouth to protest, to tell Natalie to leave her alone, but the words caught in her throat. She gasped for air, clutching the edge of her desk as the world around her swam. Her vision blurred for a moment, and she could feel her heart pounding against her ribcage. Her breath came in shallow, desperate gasps, and she squeezed her eyes shut, trying to steady herself.

Natalie took a step forward, her expression softening, but her voice remained firm. "Rose, what the hell is going on? You're scaring me. You need help—this isn't just exhaustion."

"I'm fine," Rose managed to choke out, though the words felt like they were being pulled from her through a storm. She opened her eyes and locked them onto Natalie's. "Please, don't tell anyone. I don't want anyone making a fuss." Natalie looked taken aback, and Rose could see the worry deep in her eyes.

"Why? Rose, you need help. You're not okay."

Rose shook her head vigorously. "No. No hospitals, no machines, no drama. I just need... I just need a minute, okay? Just give me a minute." She felt the pressure in her chest intensify, and she fought to suppress the panic rising in her throat. Natalie opened her mouth to argue, but Rose shot her a glare—one that, though weak, still carried the sharpness of her usual confidence.

Natalie hesitated, then let out a slow breath, clearly torn. She knew better than to push too hard when Rose was this stubborn. "Alright," Natalie said quietly. "I'm not going anywhere, though. If you need anything, let me know. I'll stay right here."

Rose gave a small nod, her hands still gripping the chair arms, her fingers turning white from the pressure. The air around her felt suffocating. She wanted to scream, to rip her chest open and let in all the air. She wanted to do something to make it stop, but all she could do was sit there, trying to hold onto the fragile semblance of control.

Natalie stayed by her side, not pushing and not leaving either. She watched Rose like a hawk, scanning her for any sign of real danger. All Rose could think about was how pathetic she must look —slouched there, unable to breathe, and unable to maintain the tough exterior she'd so carefully crafted over the years.

"I don't want to be a burden," Rose finally whispered, her voice hoarse. "I don't want anyone to know. They'll just make a big deal out of it. I don't want to be that person, Natalie. I don't want people looking at me like I'm weak."

Natalie's eyes softened, and she reached out, placing a gentle hand on Rose's shoulder. "Okay. Just between you and me. But Rose, you're not weak. You're not a burden. You don't have to do this alone, okay? I will help you."

Rose nodded weakly. She couldn't explain it —not to Natalie, not to anyone. She knew her body was failing. She could have gotten medical attention, but she was busy. Rose realized she might have been in denial and was not, in fact, invincible. There was a part of her, deep down, that hated the thought of appearing vulnerable. Her whole life had been about proving she was strong, and she didn't need anyone's pity. She was the grand dame of this joint, and the show must go on.

CHAPTER 10

The Candidate

Natalie sat at the bar with Jessica, casually wiping down glasses while she waited for the dinner rush to begin. She'd left Rose at the hostess stand once the older woman seemed to breathe easier. She felt a little guilty not telling anyone else about the incident by the hostess stand, but Natalie respected her boss too much to disobey. She could keep an eye out through the evening and maybe talk Rose into going home early.

The dim light from the overhead lamps bounced off the rich wood of the bar, creating an almost ethereal glow that highlighted the deep blue v-neck shirt and the loose strands of her blonde hair. She was a striking presence in the restaurant, often turning heads as she walked past the tables. She was used to being the center of attention, especially when she was surrounded by the type of men she normally found attractive – tall, muscular, broad-shouldered men who had that commanding presence and otherwise were useless.

She liked a man just smart enough to be fun

but not so overconfident that he mansplained or dug into her stories deeply. She was just having fun. She knew it was a little dangerous to call attention to herself, but she almost liked the risk if she was honest. Lately, her thoughts had started to drift toward someone who didn't fit her usual type, and that certain someone was named Felix.

Felix, whose name seemed to fit him perfectly, was a bit of an enigma. He wasn't at all the type of guy that would catch her attention. He was shorter, with wiry arms that looked like they belonged on a man who spent more time in front of a computer than at the gym. He had a calm, almost nerdy energy about him that was in stark contrast to her usual magnetism toward brawn.

She dismissed him initially when she started working at the Trailside. She remembered how he'd stood at the coffee counter, nervously glancing around at the other servers, trying to blend in without looking entirely out of place. He wasn't trying to be noticed like the other guys, who were always puffing out their chests or making sure they walked with a confident swagger. Felix was modest and even reserved, keeping his head down and his voice low. And oh! That voice. She'd caught herself missing it when she was not at work.

Natalie somehow was noticing him more and more. It was the little things, really—the way he carried himself with quiet competence, the way he listened when others spoke, and his unassuming sense of humor. She felt a little jealous of Maisie. The two of them laughed together so often and had endless inside jokes of which she was not a part. Like how their 'gang' was now called The Independent Trailside Society, TITS for short, since they'd learned Felix had two degrees.

The best thing lately was that he'd stopped asking her out. This let her relax and just enjoy him as a friend. He was the kind of guy who wasn't trying to impress anyone, and in that lack of effort, there was something undeniably intriguing to her.

But there were parts of her that resisted the pull. She had always been attracted to strength—physically and emotionally. Her ex-boyfriend had that rugged quality she liked. Look where the fuck that got her. Afraid for her safety, she left her one good friend and went on the run. The brute types were fun in theory, but they usually had issues. They were the types who could protect her, hold her when she felt vulnerable, and make her feel safe. They were muscle men in every sense of the word. But Felix? She didn't know if he could do any of that. He was the kind of guy who would probably avoid a physical confrontation at all costs, and his idea of a good time was more likely to involve a book or a video game than a hike through the mountains.

Why am I even thinking about this? she wondered. Natalie turned away from the counter and wiped a few more glasses, her mind whirling.

She had always prided herself on two things this past year: her independence and her ability to control a man. She had dated athletes, guys with a certain swagger, the kind who exuded confidence. Felix was confident in a different way that was... nicer. Being a nice guy was underrated. There was also something different about the way he looked at her that Natalie liked. He wasn't mentally peeling her clothes off. It was like he saw *Her*.

She caught herself stealing a glance at him across the room. He was talking to a customer at the front, gesturing toward the menu with enthusiasm as he explained the day's special. He wasn't perfect, but she could see a certain passion in the way he spoke, the way he took his job seriously, even though it was just a waiter gig. His eyes lit up when he talked about the food, a stark contrast to his usual calm demeanor. Natalie couldn't help but find it endearing.

See? her mind argued. *That's a good quality. He's passionate. He's engaged with life. He is a nice person.* She rolled her eyes slightly at herself. She had no idea why she was overanalyzing this so much. She knew her type, and Felix wasn't it. She liked men who could lift her up with ease, who made her feel small and feminine in comparison. She was a big girl and liked a big man to make her feel dainty. Felix, on the other hand, seemed more the type to read her a book of poetry and get lost in abstract thoughts. Maybe she would like poetry? She hadn't thought about that before, not since that creative writing class during her brief stint in college.

Felix looked up at her as she watched him, and she looked up at the ceiling like an idiot. *What am I doing?* Felix looked up, too, to see what caught her eye. He gave her a quizzical look as he slipped through the kitchen door. He was as goofy as she was. Staring up at the ceiling, what was that? Ugh. She wasn't sure if she could ever feel that magnetic pull she craved with someone like him.

Then again, there was a subtle charm about him. He had a way of making her feel seen in a way that the muscle-bound guys never had. When they talked, it wasn't just surface-level banter. It was real, meaningful conversation. She had noticed that he asked questions—not the typical "What do you like to do for fun?" nonsense, but thoughtful inquiries that showed he genuinely cared about getting to know her. No one had ever really asked her about her dreams, her ambitions, or her past in quite the same way.

He also remembered what she said. She'd lamented that the restaurant didn't have little cocktail umbrellas for drinks, and the next time they were all lounging around the bar after work, a bright green umbrella was plopped in her glass. Maisie, Jessica and even Chip were jealous, so he became King of the Hill, passing them out so everyone could have one. It was...disarming.

Natalie folded a white cloth napkin with a little more force than necessary as she tried to reason with herself. *He's not the type who could take charge in a difficult situation,* she thought. *He's not someone who would throw himself in front of danger or stand tall when the world is crashing down around him.*

As if on cue, Felix walked by, holding a tray of drinks for a table. He smiled at her, a small, warm smile that made her heart skip a beat. He didn't seem to know that she was having an internal struggle over his mere existence. It didn't matter. For a brief moment, she caught a glimpse of something that made her question all her previous assumptions.

He wasn't like the other guys—he wasn't physically strong, but at that moment, Natalie realized he had a quiet strength about him that she hadn't noticed before. He carried himself with grace, with ease, never trying too hard, never pushing. He seemed comfortable in his own skin.

Wasn't that what she really wanted? To be with someone who was self-assured, not because they had muscles or looks to back it up, but because they were secure in who they were? Her internal dialogue shifted. *Maybe muscles aren't everything,* she thought, feeling an unfamiliar sense of openness to the idea. *Maybe Felix has something that the other guys don't.*

It wasn't that she had to give up everything she loved about physicality in men—she still liked the idea of someone who could sweep her off her feet in a literal and metaphorical sense. After all her efforts to protect herself from men, there was room for something different. Maybe, in the quiet moments with Felix, she could find a new kind of attraction—one that depended on brains, warmth, and a shared connection.

As she looked up at him again, this time more openly, she couldn't help but smile. She enjoyed his friendship and loved his rumbling voice. There was something about him that began to draw her in slowly.

CHAPTER 11

Anyone Can See I Love You

Felix's hands gripped the steering wheel of his car a little tighter as he neared the turn onto her street. The familiar stretch of road felt almost foreign tonight, as if it were some unknown path leading him to an entirely new life. A possibility he had always known was there, and never fully acknowledged. He had been down this street hundreds of times before, yet tonight it seemed like the most important journey upon which he had ever embarked.

His heart hammered in his chest, every beat punctuated with a mix of nervous energy and an anticipation that he could barely contain. He glanced in the rearview mirror, running a hand through his dark hair, trying to smooth away the sweat that had formed along his hairline. He wasn't sure if it was the heat of the evening or the simmering excitement that had taken hold of him. Probably both. The thought of what was waiting for him, just around the corner, made him feel like a teenager again—vulnerable and electric all at once.

Natalie.

Her name echoed in his head, a constant, almost rhythmic thought that would not leave him alone. Tonight, they would finally hang out alone! He looked up at the big house. He knew she was out there, somewhere in her house, waiting. She had always been so mysterious to him, so intriguing. When she first walked into the restaurant all those months ago, he had known there was something about her that captivated him. She had a presence, a sort of quiet confidence that immediately drew him to her. He had found himself watching and studying her subconsciously. He always wondered what she was really like behind that cool, almost aloof facade.

At work, they shared small moments, brief exchanges that had made him more and more curious about who she really was. Every time he tried to get closer, she had shut him down. It had stung, of course. The rejection each time had been a quiet blow, but it was never harsh. There was never any cruelty in her words, just a soft, polite refusal. The smile she imparted always had a sense of distance. She had always been kind and never anything more than that. He knew deep down there was something more there—something she wasn't ready to reveal, something that was waiting. He could feel it in the way she glanced at him sometimes, in the small, fleeting moments when her guard slipped ever so slightly.

Tonight, he was determined to break

through it. He couldn't ignore it anymore—the undeniable connection, the pull between them that neither of them could pretend didn't exist. She was still guarded, but he had a feeling tonight would be different. Something told him she would finally open up, maybe not all at once, but enough for him to understand who she really was.

The car rolled to a stop in front of the big house, and for a moment, Felix simply stared at the gate he knew led to the small pool house where she lived. He took a moment to ogle the huge house, wondering what her landlord was like. In one of the upper rooms, he could see the faint outline of someone moving inside, maybe just a shadow. The landlord was home tonight. He looked past the gate, towards Natalie's place. He got out of the car and headed up the driveway. The feeling in his chest swelled with a mixture of excitement and nerves. This was it. He could almost hear the breathless voice in his head whispering, *This is your chance. Don't fuck it up.*

He took a deep breath, trying to steady himself. He had worked himself up for this night. No one else could make it, thank God. He had made sure everything was right—he had brushed off his nerves earlier and had gotten himself into a place where he felt ready to be alone with her, without hesitation. He just had to remind himself that they had spent so much time around each other already. There was a familiarity in her presence, even if she had always kept him at a distance.

They worked together, day in and day out, their shifts blending into one another, yet they barely ever spoke outside the normal routine of the restaurant. The moments they had shared – those tiny, unspoken exchanges – had always felt significant. He knew he was right. She wasn't as simple as she pretended to be. What was that line from one of Shakespeare's plays? "All the world's a stage; And all the men and women merely players." Felix was determined to have Natalie drop that facade tonight and be real for once. Tonight, he hoped, was the night he would get to the heart of her. With shaky hands, he grabbed his phone and texted her: *I'm outside your house.*

Her reply came almost instantly: *Creepy! See you in a sec.* It was funny, freewheeling, just like her. Felix loved it, even if it drove him a little crazy sometimes. He wondered, as he put his phone down and got out of the car, if she had ever let her guard down completely. Surely that false front, the dumb blonde routine, got old? Maybe tonight, he could help her drop her disguise to reveal her own version of 'Rosalind'.

He walked toward the gate, his footsteps louder in his ears than they probably should have been. His hands were slick with sweat now. He had been invited here, and he still didn't feel like he fully belonged. He'd been here a few times before, but those had been casual visits with the gang, not like this. Tonight felt different.

When she opened the door, his breath

caught in his throat. She was standing there in the doorway, framed by the soft light from inside, her blonde hair cascading down her back in waves that made his heart skip a beat. She wore something simple—black leggings and a loose pinkish sweater—but to him, she looked like she had stepped out of some kind of dream. She gave him a small smile, and for the first time, it didn't feel like a wall between them. It felt like an invitation.

"Hey," she said softly, her voice like honey, as always. "Come in." She was out of breath. As he stepped inside, his eyes couldn't help but scan the room. It was cozy, a reflection of her—warm, inviting, with an underlying layer of something he couldn't quite place. It wasn't perfect, but that was part of its charm. It felt comfortable and like it had its own history.

"You look nice," he said, trying to sound casual, though his voice betrayed him, trembling just slightly. Her lips quirked, a half-smile.

"Thanks," she replied, almost shyly, before stepping aside to allow him entry. "I have Guiness for you!" She busied herself at the kitchen counter, getting them both a pint glass from the freezer this time, he noticed.

"Great. I see the landlord is home tonight." Was he just imagining it, or did she look startled? It was hard to tell from someone's back.

"No, they are out of town, I'm sure." She turned towards him, a frosty beer in each hand.

Why was she saying they weren't home? He'd seen a light on, and someone had been moving around on the second floor. He decided to let it drop. His mother wisely taught that a person could be right or happy, but rarely could they be both.

She joined him on the couch, and soon, the air between them became charged with an energy that neither of them had quite acknowledged before. The silence stretched for a moment, thick and almost uncomfortable. Felix didn't let it linger for long.

"I've been wanting to ask you something," he began, his voice quieter than he had intended. "You're not like... the other people at Trailside." She raised an eyebrow with interest. She hadn't responded, but he could see the shift in her eyes, a flicker of something. He wasn't sure what it was, yet he knew it was there. He leaned forward slightly, his voice low, as if sharing a secret. "There's more to you than you let on, isn't there?"

Her eyes darkened, and he could see the hesitation on her face. It was almost as if she had been expecting the question, or maybe she was just afraid of where it might lead. "Maybe," she said, her voice betraying none of the emotion she must have been feeling.

Felix smiled, determined. "I think you're smarter than you let on. Smarter than anyone suspects."

She stiffened. Her eyes didn't leave his. He

could tell something in her was starting to shift. He just had to wait for it; just had to be patient. Something told him tonight that he would finally be able to reach the real her. "Well, I don't have two freaking degrees like you do, Felix!" They both laughed.

The TITS gang had been mocking him daily for his excessive education for someone waiting tables. Felix thought most people had layers to them. One of his layers happened to be his education and interest in poetry and literature. What were Natalie's layers?

Natalie didn't open up like he hoped she would. The rest of their evening was good. He tried to act like a good friend instead of the pining, lovesick puppy he actually was. He left after the beer dregs grew warm, not wanting to overstay his welcome. He whistled down the driveway, mentally celebrating a perfectly normal evening between them.

CHAPTER 12

Bus Stop

Summer was finally in full bloom in the small town of Valparaiso. The downtown splash pad was crowded with parents and little kids of every age from late morning until afternoon nap time. Natalie often drove downtown for coffee or to have lunch at one of the many awesome places within a few blocks of downtown's main square. She'd shop for gifts or little flourishes for her home at Lifestyles gift shop, pick up a decadent box of crispy chewy macarons from Bao's French Bakery, or simply sit on a Central Park Plaza bench with a flimsy tortilla like pizza from Rolling Stonebaker's carry-out window.

She could spend several hours wandering downtown on her own, but sometimes, she missed having a girlfriend with her. Her closest friend in years was the one she shouldn't think about now. She just wanted to send a text to Dori to make sure she was okay. She also wanted to ask about him to make sure no one had traced who Natalie used to be and who she was now. It was all impossible. She had to let Dori go to keep her safe.

She smiled as she basked in the sun, the cries and giggles of the splash pad fading as she thought of the friend she lost. They had met as beer bitches at Shelter, a dark, hidden nightclub on Waveland. Dori had the most beautiful smile and smoky, mysterious eyes. She took more tips in than any other server because she gave as much shit back as any patron could give. Her sexy confidence and no-bullshit personality earned her respect, oodles of phone numbers, tips, and hot kisses.

They had called her special customers "The Harem" because there were so many of them. Natalie laughed as she daydreamed on the bench, remembering a time Dori rescued her from a handsy guest who was out of control. Dori reached between them, grabbed the loser by the balls, and squeezed gently as she smiled. "I think you need to go home or go to jail; your call." The douchebag human stuttered and seated, appearing to sober immediately. He left the moment she released him, and Dori made sure Natalie was okay and delivered the beer she held in the other hand to another patron. Dori wasn't someone others worried about, and that might have been what got her into trouble.

"Hey, Loser." Natalie shook herself from the memory and blinked up at the person in front of her. The pink hair was out of place, but she'd know that rough voice anywhere now.

"Maisie!" The girl plopped on the bench next to her, helping herself to the last slice of pizza.

"What are you doing here?"

"I don't work till four, so like you, just enjoying Valpo." Maisie chewed with her mouth open, smacking her lips and grinning at Natalie. "How was your date the other night?" Natalie wasn't sure what she meant. Since her dalliance with Thor, she hadn't bothered dating at all. He was at the bar several times a week, so if she wanted another run at him, he was available.

Maisie clarified, "Felix was over, you know, the cute dude we work with?"

Natalie took a deep breath in and blew it out, rolling her eyes. "Maisie, you know we are just friends. It wasn't a date." Natalie sipped from her water bottle, startled, and continued, "Wait! Did he say it was a date?"

Maisie shook her head. "Nope. He didn't say a thing. I just knew about it. There's just something about you that people respond to."

Natalie smiled and her eyes widened, waiting. "Would you like to know my secret?"

Maisie nodded, leaning in. She was a cute girl but crass. Maybe she needed some tips. Natalie smiled and said, "I finally decided to like myself. I decided to put myself first. I decided to say what I wanted to say and do what I wanted to do instead of waiting for permission or approval."

"But it doesn't hurt that you are gorgeous, Nat."

"Aw, thanks girl. I think it is mostly my attitude. I believe that's what they're responding to. The fact that I don't give any fucks and I love myself." Maise leaned towards her, pulling a blonde lock of her hair to twirl around her finger in a cozy move. Natalie slipped her arm around the girl's slim shoulders and gave her a little hug.

"He's crazy about you, you know?"

At Maisie's words, Natalie slumped against the bench, nodding. "Yeah, I turned him down a bunch of times when I first started at TITS. I think he knows now I only want friendship."

Maisie pulled her legs up on the bench, practically squatting like a goblin beside her. "Do you? I have eyes, you know. I see you looking for him, and I know he's got it bad for you."

Natalie turned to face Maisie, shuffling her bottle against the bench between them. Some kid hollered, "MMMMMaaaaMAAAAAA!" Making them both turn for a moment, looking for blood and finding none.

"I like him, sure. Felix is a good person. I just don't have time for... complications in my life." Natalie met Maisie's eyes and the dubious expression on her elfin face.

"How busy is a woman working as a server? You got secret agent stuff I don't know about?"

Natalie sat stiffly and let her eyes drift to the people dotted around the park. "I mean, I don't want a relationship. What I need...Thor provides."

Maisie gagged and laughed at the same time, making a weird, snorgling sound that made Natalie's head turn to her in alarm. "Thor would be good for that, I suppose." Maisie stretched out on her half of the bench. "Not that I'd know."

They sat in silence for a while. A wayward frisbee almost clocked her in the face, but she picked it up and flung it back to its owner. The sun beat down on their skin as they watched the crowd ebb and flow. The scent of sunscreen, pizza, and joy hung in the air around them.

Maisie finally stood to leave, "You oughta give him a real chance, Nat." Her voice was soft, with none of her trademark sarcasm. The tenderness made the message hang in the air between them. Natalie let her eyes fall to her lap, nodding once. When she looked up again, Maisie was halfway across the park, her words left behind.***

Sometimes, she just wanted to go to the grocery store unnoticed. She'd wear cut-off shorts and a sweatshirt. The sweatshirt wouldn't be off the shoulder, and maybe she wouldn't put on lipstick. She would just wander through the store doing her grocery shopping. Other times, when she wanted to be noticed, she would raise her energy. She would send out a 'come hither' vibe. She would roll her hips as she sauntered down the aisles. She would slide the same sweatshirt just off the shoulder a little bit, and all of a sudden, everyone around her would be smiling and paying attention to her. It was magic, the way she could turn her appeal, her magnetism, on or off depending on her desires. She'd read about

Marilyn Monroe doing the same thing, and she felt they were just two dumb blondes in a secret club together.

Sometimes, she would do it just to make sure she still could. Sure, her looks and her curvaceous body helped, but the real magic was at the center of who she was and who she chose to be in the world. She was kind of glad other people didn't know how to do it. She didn't share this with Maisie because she knew it would sound arrogant and conceited.

She hadn't been intentionally trying to hook Felix, but over the months, she had started to like him. He'd grown on her as a friend. She liked his sense of humor and the subtle way he moved through Trailside. The rest of the TITS gang seemed to defer to his ideas and seek out his opinions. She admired him a lot now that she knew him. She had wondered what it might be like to kiss him.

He'd been dressing better, with lots of dark-colored henleys with a few buttons undone and dark rinse jeans, and he'd either slimmed down a little or bulked up...she'd noticed his biceps pressing against his shirt when he carried trays and thought it was kind of hot. He was smart, and that could be a problem, but he wasn't jealous, controlling, or into illegal activities. Maybe she was ready for a nice guy after all these years.

She was glad to have Maisie as a friend, and she continued to miss Dori. It wasn't safe to reach out, so Dori would have to stay in her past. Anything between them also linked them to the one person she never wanted to see again.

Natalie spent the afternoon cleaning the big house, fantasizing about calling Dori, catching up. She vacuumed the halls upstairs and Swiffered the vast wood floors downstairs. She had earbuds blasting the Ocean's Eleven Soundtrack and danced as she worked. She could hire someone to do this, but it was one of the times she really enjoyed the big house. Cleaning what was hers, what she earned, felt even better than buying it. Decorating it was fun, but the pool house is where she felt the most at home.

In the big house's main bedroom, she had placed a huge California king bed with a down comforter, Egyptian cotton sheets, and too many fluffy pillows. The bedroom was painted a warm pinkish grey which made her skin look radiant. The bedding was all navy blue in various patterns and shades. The curtains were a heavy grey that shone, and the bedroom furniture looked like something straight out of a 1940 Hollywood starlet's boudoir. It was art deco with a pewter finish that looked almost metallic. The dresser and nightstands had mirrors on the front panels and down the legs.

Natalie had found a mirrored chandelier with crystals and silver dangly bits, and it was the eye-catcher in the center of the room. She'd put down impractical but luscious sheepskin rugs and had a blue velvet upholstered bench at the foot of the bed. She'd spent a huge amount of money making this room fit for a queen. Instead of regal, though, she felt hollow in it. She loved running her hands over the beautiful things, but she slept in the pool house more nights than not.

CHAPTER 13

Wine and Roses

"Psycho Killer" by Talking Heads blares through the Toyota's speakers, making them vibrate desperately with the overpowering beat. He holds the grey sweatshirt in his lap and it is against his nose so he can breathe in her perfume before he realizes it. *Dumbass. What are you doing? She is gonna see right through this.* His self-talk does nothing to turn the car around.

"I'm just a friend returning a sweatshirt." He spoke aloud as if the car might respond. At last, he turns onto her street and pulls up to the house. The lights are on, the landlord must be home. He sniffs the grey pile bunched in his hand one last time before exiting his vehicle.

As he walks up the driveway, heading straight for the pool gate, he wonders if she'll invite him to stay for lunch. Maybe a swim? *Gosh, I forgot my swimsuit...* He chuffs to himself and begins to get a semi, thinking of swimming naked in Natalie's pool. *Get it together, Loser.* He thinks to himself as he turns on the path to knock on the door of the pool house.

The pool house is dark, and there is no sign of Natalie inside, near the pool or in the garden. He shifts from foot to foot, knocking, waiting, and fighting the urge to smell her sweatshirt again. Her perfume smells rich, like a department store. Like a woman. Most of the girls he knew wore sweet smells or fruity body sprays, and far too much of them. Natalie was all woman and always seemed luxurious, even in jeans and a shirt. There was something about her that–

"Felix?" He whirled towards the patio of the mansion and saw Natalie hustling towards him, out of breath and worried. "What are you doing here? Did you text me?" She reached behind her for her cell phone, not finding it in the tiny pockets of her sundress.

He stood dumbly, staring at her. She was so goddamn gorgeous. Her hair was falling out of a messy bun, and her tiny sundress floated around her tanned legs as she came to a stop in front of him. Her brow was furrowed as she waited for him to explain himself. "I... Uh. Oh! I brought you your sweatshirt." He thrust it into her hands with a smile, trying to get his shit together.

She took the item, and they stood there in the late afternoon sun. Birds were literally singing as he stood, just looking at her. How could she look both sweet and seductive at the same time? Her body was so curvy he struggled not to let his eyes roam over it.

"Thank you." She said, finally. She caught

her breath and offered a big sigh.

"Why were you there and not here?" He points first at the huge house behind them, then to the pool house they stood beside.

He watched her face form several replies, and she said at last,"Wine! I ran out. They don't care if I borrow from them, so that is what I was doing." She laughed awkwardly.

Felix knew he shouldn't push, but he was a curious fellow. If there was a button that said Do Not Push, Felix McCall would be first in line to push it. The moment something was off limits, it was his goal. His second bachelor's degree was part of that. He'd been interested in a woman taking classes he wasn't, and then he got so interested in the classes he just added the Psychology degree to his own goals. He never went out with the girl, but he got another degree. "Where is the wine, then?"

He watched Natalie blink slowly and shape a coy grin onto her lips. It looked fake and made her less attractive at that moment. He waited to see what she would say, enjoying the small sense of power he suddenly had in their dynamic. She looked at her hands holding nothing but the sweatshirt he'd just handed her. "They were out."

"Out?" Felix raised his eyebrows, a look of mock horror on his face.

"Yup," she rocked back on her heels. She looked him right in the eye, serious.

"That big 'ol house prolly has a wine cellar, but they are out?" He offered her a wide-eyed smile, and she stared at him, likely incredulous at his doubt.

She turned to look behind them at the house, as if she'd never seen it before. "Yeah. Crazy, huh? Fucking alcoholics." She laughed and took him by the arm. "I'm gonna have to get my own wine, I guess. Wanna do a Target run?"

His foolish heart leaped as she took his arm and steered him towards the garden path and the gate beyond that. "Might you need shoes? A Purse? I don't think Target lets just anyone in these days. It is quite a place." He heard her gasp and chuckle.

She shoved him playfully forward. "Go to your car; I'll be there in a sec."

She turned away from him towards the path back to the pool house. He listened to her bare feet padding as she ran, and he retraced his steps to spy on her. He watched her pass the pool house door and continue to the big house. He shook his head and headed to his car to wait for her.

Why was she lying about where she lived? Did she actually live in that huge house? Why did Natalie seem so open and friendly one moment and then closed off the next? This beautiful woman was an endless ocean to discover. Would she ever trust him enough to let him know who she really was?

***

"This is my happy place!" Natalie crowed as she grabbed a red plastic cart. The bright lights above buzzed softly in Target's aisles, casting a shopping frenzy-inducing glow over the shelves stacked with everything a person could want. Everywhere they looked, brightly labeled items were waiting for discovery.

"Isn't it everyone's happy place?" He asked. Felix stood before the wine section, his fingers lightly trailing along the rows. Being here with Natalie made the ordinary act of buying wine feel a little more thrilling.

Natalie caught up to him in the store after a beauty aisle detour. He saw she was a little out of breath, sundress swirling around her legs in that mesmerizing way. With a glance back at the selection of wines, he wheeled his cart toward her, the smooth sound of the wheels against the polished floor loud to his ears. Did he really need a cart? They just came for a bottle of wine, right?

"Hey, you're here for the wine too?" he asked, a playful smile tugging at the corner of his lips. He couldn't help but notice how her shining blonde hair framed her face in waves and how she seemed to glow even under the harsh store lights.

Oh God, was he a goner for this girl? Yes. All kinds of a goner.

Natalie glanced over her shoulder at him, her green eyes sparking with amusement. "Is that a serious question? Of course. I mean, it's Target. You don't come here for the décor." She gave a small, teasing laugh, her voice warm and inviting. "Unless you're planning to buy something from the dollar section?"

Felix chuckled, his eyes scanning the shelves for an excuse to stay close. "I'm actually more of a beer guy, but…" He shrugged dramatically, "A good deal on candles is hard to resist."

"Ooh! So you're a man of mystery," Natalie said, her voice dipping into a playful tone, and for a moment, her hand lingered over a bottle of Merlot as if she was considering it. "But I'll let you in on a secret. I'm here for something a little less… sophisticated." She picked up a bottle of Stella Rosa with a sly smile, holding it up to the light. "This one. It's my favorite." She put two bottles into the cart beside a carton of milk and some Mr. Bubble.

Felix raised an eyebrow, intrigued by her confidence. "Less sophisticated, huh? I'm intrigued. What makes you say that? The wine or your taste in it?" He took a small step closer, careful not to invade her space but clearly enjoying the proximity.

Natalie glanced at him, noting the playful glint in his eyes. "Oh, both," she teased, her voice low, almost conspiratorial. "Stella is sweet and fizzy and a little bit edgy but still smooth. Kind of like someone who knows what they want. Not afraid to take a risk and have some fun."

Felix smirked, intrigued by the way she spoke. She had an effortless charm. There was something deeper in her words that felt a little more daring. "Sounds like someone I'd like to get to know," he said, leaning just a touch closer, his gaze flicking to the bottle in her hand. "But tell me, what does that make you?"

Natalie held his gaze for a beat longer than necessary, letting the tension hang in the air between them. Then, with a playful flick of her wrist, she put the bottle back on the shelf. "I think I'm more of a... mystery. You know, the kind of wine you taste and immediately wish you knew more about it. Besides, I very much like the labels more so than just the wine inside."

Felix's lips curled into a grin. "I'm intrigued." She was flirting! She was really, finally flirting with him. "Do you prefer red wine?" His voice was light, and he realized his mistake almost immediately.

"I'm open to anything. Whatever looks good tastes good in the moment, you know?" She leaned in conspiratorially, "Are we doing the Schitt's Creek wine label scene right now? I adore that show!"

"Uh, no. I mean, yeah, it is a good scene." He paused, unsure of how to proceed.

"Oh my God. Do you not know Schitt's Creek?" Her body lost its flirty energy, and she stood studying him.

"Of course, I know it. I do know it. I know it too well. My– well, Rose at work is obsessed."

Natalie let out a long sigh-groan-aha sound. "Oh! That is it! Rose sounds like Moira Rose!"

"Yeah." Felix didn't seem as excited about it as she was.

The blonde practically jumped up and down

in the wine aisle. "That has been bugging me since I met her...the voice, the wigs, I couldn't place it. Duh. So obvious."

"Yeah, she legally changed her name to Rose when the show wrapped up." Felix grinned at Rose's commitment. She'd always been dramatic and now she had a persona.

There was a long pause as they both stood there, each silently weighing the other. The air between them was charged with something unspoken, something new and exciting. Natalie finally broke the silence, glancing at a bottle of Cabernet Sauvignon. "What about this one? You think it has the same kind of mystique?"

Felix glanced at the bottle, then at her. "Hmm. A little too... obvious for my taste. Cabernet is bold, confident, and maybe even a little overpowering. If you're looking for something that makes a statement, then sure, it's your pick. If you want something that lingers, leaves you wanting more..." He trailed off, his eyes locking with hers. "You'd probably go for something like this." He grabbed a bottle of Pinot Noir and held it up, smiling knowingly.

"Pinot Noir, huh? Subtle. I can see that. So, what are you saying? That you're into subtlety?" Natalie asked, her voice playful, yet the question carried a weight that was hard to ignore.

Felix met her gaze, the corners of his lips curving upwards. "I'm into whatever keeps me coming back for more," he replied smoothly, his tone lowering just slightly, the words almost a challenge.

Natalie felt her heart race a little faster. There was no denying the chemistry between them anymore. It crackled in the air like static. "And what if I should need to come back for more?" she asked, stepping just a little closer.

"Depends," he said, his eyes gleaming with mischief. "What would you bring to the table?"

Natalie looked surprised and offended. Then her smile deepened as she leaned in just a fraction more. "I'd bring good conversation, a bottle of something nice, and maybe..." She trailed off, her voice soft and inviting, "Maybe a kiss. Only if you're worth it."

Felix's breath caught in his throat for a split second, but he didn't back down. Instead, he reached for a bottle of Chardonnay. "Kisses, huh?" His goddamn voice cracked like a middle schooler's. He took a deep breath and tried again. "Well, let's just say I prefer someone who knows how to keep a good thing going. Like a great Chardonnay—smooth, not too bold, but something you can savor." Felix's eyes never left hers as he placed the Chardonnay back on the shelf.

"I think I can manage that," she said, her voice low, almost a whisper. "Maybe I should take you out for that glass of wine to see if it's as good as you say."

Felix stepped back a little, his expression

playful yet teasing. "I don't know if you're ready for me," he said with a wink, his words lingering in the air between them.

Natalie raised an eyebrow, her lips curling into a half-smile. "I think I can handle it," she said, confident but still carrying that undercurrent of mystery. "You surprise me, though."

Their eyes locked again, and for a moment, the world around them seemed to vanish. They were standing close enough that he could feel the warmth of her body and hear the soft rustle of her dress, but neither of them moved to break the spell.

Felix's gaze flickered down to her lips before meeting her eyes again, and it was clear they were both thinking the same thing.

"I think we'll find out soon enough," she whispered, her voice husky, teasing. Her eyes sparkled with something more than just playful banter now. There was an undeniable energy in the air, the kind that made everything feel electric like they were on the verge of something exciting, something more than just friendship.

Felix's lips parted as he took another step closer, but just as he was about to speak, the sound of a cart behind them interrupted the moment. Both of them turned, the spell momentarily broken, but their connection was undeniable.

"Maybe another time?" Natalie said, her voice barely more than a whisper, eyes still locked on his.

Felix's lips curled into a soft, knowing smile. "Maybe. I'll see you around, then."

With that, he turned away, the soft clomp of his shoes a reminder that the night was far from over. Natalie watched him go, a smile on her face and the thought of what might happen next filling her mind.

"Dude." She huffed at him incredulously. "You drove me here."

"Well, grab some wine and catch up, Natalie!"

He winked and strolled away from the blonde.

She laughed and did just that.

It was only a matter of time.

***

They kept up the flirty talk all the way back to her house. He struggled to keep his eyes on the road with his mind already jumping ahead to kissing Natalie tonight wherever the fuck she lived. He really wanted to ask her if she really lived in the poolhouse or the big mansion house in front of it. Something was really weird here. He couldn't ask tonight, though, not if he wanted to kiss her. That was definitely his priority.

When he pulled up to the house and headed up the driveway, Natlie's phone pinged for a text message, and she paused to glance at the screen. Puzzled, she handed the bag of groceries to him to use both hands to open the message from

UNKNOWN CALLER.

Felix watched her as she read the text, the color draining from her face. She looked shocked, scared, and very, very small. He stood without speaking, stupidly holding her bags and waiting to be acknowledged.

"Um, I can't hang out now, Felix." She reached for her bags and looked furtively up and down the street. Was she looking for someone? The person who texted?

"Who is it?" His own voice sounded lame to him. There wasn't anything else to say if he didn't want to leave. She just shook her head, lifting tear-filled eyes to his.

"You need to go." She turned to hurry up to the gate and through it. He followed her, worried because she looked scared. His body was on alert, wanting to protect her from whatever this trouble was.

"What is going on, Natalie? I'm here if you need me." He stood helplessly inside the gate, looking around to make sure she got inside safely.

She turned to him, a bitter smile on her lips. "No, Felix, you cannot help me. I have to help myself." When she realized he wouldn't leave, she continued, "I am fine. I can deal with this. I will see you tomorrow at Trailside, okay?"

Without another word, she headed straight to the back patio doors of the big house, offering him only a shrug as she unlocked the sliding door and let herself inside without another backward glance.

He stood stupidly there by the kidney-shaped pool, breathing in the chlorine smell and trying to piece everything together without success. He looked around the backyard as if the answer was standing there. After staring at the door she'd disappeared through for far too long, he headed back to his own car and drove home alone.

What an awful turn of events. What the hell just happened?

CHAPTER 14

There's No Business Like Show Business

It was business as usual at Trailside the next morning. Rose sat in the corner of the bar, going over paperwork. She watched as her restaurant family worked hard on the finishing touches before lunch began. The matriarch sipped guiltily at her gin and tonic. She knew ten o'clock in the morning was too early, but damn it if her chest hadn't been bothering her. A drink made her relax.

She swiped the blonde waves back from her cheek and took another sip. She thought this wig was probably too long. It was already annoying her and the day had barely begun. Rose watched as her son took care of business and noticed that he kept looking for someone. Rose knew that someone was Natalie. She thought they had gone out the night before. She had texted him, asking him to run an errand for her, and he explained that he was at Target with the girl. Rose was delighted.

Since Natalie started at Trailside, Felix seemed to bloom at last. He let Mouthy Maisie take him shopping for new clothes, shocking them all. Last month, he moved out of the house and into a studio apartment of his own in downtown Valparaiso. He seemed more confident and healthy than she had seen him in the past few years. She knew enough not to ask about it or compliment him. He could not stop Rose from watching. Would her dear boy at last get the girl of his dreams?

Maisie carried empty bar trays to Jessica behind the bar, and Rose called out, "Maisie?" The pink-haired woman scurried over to her, eyeing the drink with its tell-tale lime twist. She said nothing. "Where is Natalie?"

Maisie looked around as if expecting her to suddenly appear. "Dunno, haven't seen her yet today. Whatcha need, Boss?"

Rose waved her away. "Nothing, just wondered if you knew." Her chest clenched again with that searing pain, and Rose gasped audibly.

Maisie stepped to her with alarm on her face. "Rose?"

Rose shook her head, trying to arrange her features and breath. "Wrong pipe." She gestured to the drink. Maisie looked at the untouched glass and back at Rose. She could be confused all she wanted as long as she left. Rose dipped her face back to her paperwork, tense and struggling to appear normal. She saw Maisie's Converse-clad feet slowly back up, and she finally sipped small bits of air into her damn lungs.

These attacks happened almost every day,

and she was scared. She was not scared enough to go see the vultures that pretended to be doctors, but she knew her situation was not good. She would have to talk to her son soon. He needed to prepare.

She wished she had cigarettes. Why did smoking have to go out of fashion? It was sexy and cool until The Trailside Team hassled her into quitting the last time she had a health scare. She wasn't desperate enough to puff on those foolish-looking vape things. A real cigarette was the best, especially if she had one of those holders like Audrey in Breakfast at Tiffany's. But no. She quit two years ago. One of her many foolish life choices.

Damn.

CHAPTER 15

Two Little Girls from Little Rock

UNKNOWN CALLER: *We need to talk. Call me.*

Natalie's chest squeezed like it might be a heart attack. Unknown caller? So few people had this new number. Even the robocalls hadn't caught it yet. Maisie, Jessica, Felix and Rose. And Thor, AKA Tom. GrubHub. They were all labeled on her phone. The weird text felt...menacing.

ZIDLER: *who is this*

She watched for the floating dots to indicate a response, but her phone screen was quiet in her hands. She tossed the phone onto the kitchen island, ignoring her sweet new friends' waiting messages. She went to the huge subzero fridge and pulled a new bottle of Stella Rosa out. The gorgeous wine bubbled in the glass, calling to her. The fizz tickled her nose as she drank several long gulps from the huge crystal goblet. She checked the phone again. There was no reply.

Natalie reached across the island, pressing her red-painted toes against the bar stool foot rail as she stretched, fingers splayed until she could grab the corner of her laptop. She slugged more wine and opened an incognito browser. Finally, after months of fighting the temptation, she reached out to Dori. She had to know.

To: DContrary@gmail.com
From: Catpants2001@hotmail.com
Sorry to reach out, but I hope you are doing well. I miss the hell out of you.
Is he alive? I got a weird text today.
Please reply asap.
Xxxx
Nancy

To: Catpants2001@hotmail.com
From: DContrary@gmail.com

OMG I MISS THE FUCK OUT OF YOU BITCH. Oh God I wondered how you were, or ...
where you were. Are you ok ? One of his boys tracked me down a month after you left asking lots of fucking questions and handed me a WAD of cash. I wasn't gonna take it but rent ya know? I think they were scared I'd go to the cops about everything. It was too awkward for me to ask about him.
Where are you? I'm doing tables

at Fifi's now. Shelter had too many memories. I've been partying too much but yolo.
Xoxo Dori

Natalie just stared at the email, missing her friend, but she knew she couldn't reconnect with her wild pal anymore. Too much had happened, and too much was in the air for that to be a good idea. Her eyes burned, and she swiped at them as they brimmed with tears.

She was alone.

On the run.

She was kidding herself that she could make some nice friends and maybe even fall for a nice guy only an hour away from the club scene that ruined her life in Chicago.

She slid the laptop away from her and looked around the enormous kitchen. It was beautiful, and if she cooked or baked or did anything kitchen-y, then this would be a great place. It was a far cry from how she'd lived before her app took off. Having money did let her buy a new life with beautiful things. The money did not buy her enough freedom to keep her from having to hide. She still never truly took a full, deep breath. Should she finally go to the police? Everything would be in the open, and then she could just live. She had created a little life here, but it wasn't real.

Her head felt so heavy with the deep

gut-wrenching sorrow and wine on an empty stomach. She laid her forehead against the cool marble counter and sobbed. How did this happen? It was all his fault. And Dori's. And hers. She pulled her legs up to her chin as she cried all the terror, loneliness, and anger she'd kept stifled for months. Eventually, the tears dried, leaving a throbbing headache behind.

Natalie left the lights on and climbed the thick, carpeted stairs to the master bedroom. She peeled off the sweatshirt, the sundress, and her satin bra and slipped under the heavy down comforter without washing her face or brushing her teeth. She sighed deeply in comfort, wanting to hide away from reality as long as possible.

A while later, Natalie sat up suddenly in bed, alarmed and panting in terror. She slid out of bed and ran to the alarm keypad in the upstairs hall. It was disarmed. How could she forget, especially now, after that text? She armed the system and staggered back to the cocoon of her bed. Her mind swirled sleepily, and it wasn't long before she plunged into a restless sleep, which helped her hide from life for a short while.

CHAPTER 16

Bombshell

Felix hadn't meant to corner her in the storage room. Natalie had avoided him all afternoon, and he was just worried. He saw her head back there near tears and took the chance to get her alone. He selfishly felt desperate to have her look at him the way she had the night before when they were at Target. She arrived at work late that morning, looking hungover and puffy-eyed. The typical version of Natalie that the TITS crew knew was a perfect bombshell, so her rough appearance raised eyebrows from Maisie and Jessica, too.

Natalie heard him behind her and turned slowly as if she'd expected it to be Felix. They just looked at each other for a few moments. "Can I trust you, Felix?" She asked quietly.

"Of course you can, Natalie!" He felt like taking her into his arms and just holding her. The problem was that her body language seemed to put up an electric force field, holding him back from taking action. She turned away from him, absently holding a sleeve of cups like a sword. As he came to stand beside her, she leaned against him slightly.

He handed her a crumpled napkin from his apron. She gave a half-hearted laugh and took it, dabbing under her eyes. He turned her to face him, fighting the urge to caress her sad face. "What is it, Sweetling?" Her eyes mirrored his as they widened at the endearment.

Her face changed and grew brighter. "What?" She almost smiled, and Felix felt like a kindergartener who'd just wet his pants in front of the class.

"What?" He tried to stand taller and look like nothing happened.

"What did you call me?" She tapped the end of the cup stack against her open palm. She was smiling now.

"I think I said Sweetie? Maisie calls you that all the time, yeah?"

Natalie barked out a rough laugh. "She does not. And you didn't say Sweetie; you said–like— Sweetling?"

Felix shook his head. She had put on her bombshell grin again now, and she moved differently than the girl he'd chased in here moments before. "No. Anyway, What was that text about last night? What is going on? I care about you. I am your friend, and I care, and you can trust me." He was certainly not Shakespeare, but his heart hung in his throat. *WTF was that Sweetling gobbledygook?* He was an idiot, and she would never give him a chance again.

To his surprise, she didn't leave. She studied his face and seemed to give in all at once. "I'm not a good person, Felix. I like you a lot, and I cannot keep this up without you knowing the truth." She stopped and looked around the storeroom as if she just realized where they were.

He was afraid even to breathe, worried she would remember he was just a nerdy guy who never got the girl and didn't deserve her secrets. She didn't speak for a few moments, and they both looked towards the door, hearing their coworkers scuffling and laughing as they worked.

Her sad, scared green eyes met his, and in one motion, he wrapped his arms around her and pulled her into a tight embrace. She offered zero resistance, and the moment swelled in a silent crescendo. She smelled faintly of burnt sugar and perfume. How could she look awful and still be so beautiful?

At last, he found the words and whispered them into her sweaty blonde hair. "I can handle all of you, no matter what. I mean it, Natalie. Anything." He felt her slump further into his embrace, and he wondered if he should kiss her. *Probably not.*

Instead, a moment of inspiration and bravado hit, and he took her by the hand. She gave him a look, but he felt it was a take charge and man up moment. He pulled her through the kitchen, tugged the strings on his apron, and left it behind the coffee bar. They headed to the front door.

"Do you need stuff from your locker?" She shook her head. He stopped to whisper something to Maisie, who gave them both a concerned look but nodded. Then, he turned to Natalie and confidently guided her out the front door of Trailside.

"We are outta here. Yours or mine?" She looked like she was about to cry again and shrugged. "How 'bout mine? You haven't been there yet. It's close." He guided her to his car, opened the door for her, and was grateful the car was fairly clean these days. It didn't even smell right now. Small miracles.

"Okay." Her voice was small, as if all the fight had left her body. He fought to keep his eyes on the road, and now as he ushered her into his small studio apartment, he felt overwhelmed with feelings for this woman. So far, they have become friends. Felix felt he was about to get a lot closer to Natalie Zidler.

She sunk wearily into his couch, the tan corduroy fabric embracing her curvy body like a welcome guest. She pulled a throw pillow to her chest, tightly wrapping her arms around it as she watched his movements in the small space.

"Would you like a drink?" His fucking voice cracked. It actually cracked like he was some middle school boy. Felix could die on the spot. He didn't expire, he tried again, nervous now that she was here. "I could make you a coffee, or I have Dr. Pepper or LaCroix?" He stood between the girl on his couch and the tiny excuse for a kitchen. Some mechanical thing sighed as it clicked on, making the room feel like it was breathing with them.

She looked around the small apartment from her perch on the couch. A few dirty dishes gathered beside the sink and there was the whiff of bacon in the air from his breakfast that morning. "Felix, come here, please."

He went to her, worry all over his handsome features. She noticed he'd become more attractive over the months they had become friends. He'd bought new clothes, developed more confidence, and begun working out. It was interesting to watch him evolve. She knew he was a good man. She finally admitted to herself she might just be ready for one of those. If he didn't run when he heard what she had to say.

"I guess the short story is I was dating a fragile man, and I had a greedy girlfriend.They got along better than I did with either of them." Natalie tucked her hair behind her ear, then untucked it.

"I developed an app, and it started making a lot of money very fast. My girlfriend would celebrate my accomplishments, but she also expected me to pick up the tab when she learned how much money I was making. I didn't mind. I loved her. We had been friends for a few years, and she mattered to me." Natalie uncrossed her legs and looked at Felix. He smiled tentatively and patted her shoulder to encourage her and to say more. "I noticed that she and my boyfriend, Billy, got along really well, and it seemed like they got along *too well* at some point."

Felix shifted closer to her, his face showing disdain and disbelief. "They didn't."

"They kinda did." Natalie took a swig from her glass and continued. "I was so heartbroken and so stunned. It was kind of like that scene in that one movie where he says nothing happened, and the woman just completely ignores the signs."

Natalie continued, "I decided I was never going to date a fragile man again. I wanted oafs, I wanted big guys that were dumb, and so I made a point of dating waiters, no offense, or guys at the weightlifting section of the gym. Men that want to fuck and that's about it. I don't have to worry about whether they're after me or my money if I don't get to know them very well." The blonde had tears in her eyes as she studied Felix for his reaction.

He tried not to be distracted by her perfume, her vulnerability. He knew his role was as a friend. He cared enough to keep his hands to himself. This was serious, and he cared about the woman beside him. "Please, go on Nat."

She nodded and stretched out her legs again. Her body sank into his soft couch as she continued. "I don't tell anyone about my money. As you know, I live as if I don't have any. I did not intend to have friends. I chose to be alone and thought maybe I'd get a cat or something because they're at least obvious about their natures. They want food. They want water. They want affection when they want it. They don't have ulterior motives or secrets or bullshit. Animals are better than people. So, I date dumb men. I chose not to have any friends until y'all fucked that up."

They sat for a while, her words hanging in the air between them. Felix felt there was more, but he knew his luck might run out if he pushed her. He was a patient man. He waited.

Natalie spoke up again, her voice stronger. She didn't look at Felix. "The text the other night was from some bad people from my past. They are... maybe looking for me."

He moved closer to her, put a hand on her leg, and quickly moved to her shoulder to avoid impropriety. "Why?"

"I used to work in a club as a dancer."

"Oh my God! A stripper?" The words were out before he realized what he was saying.

Natalie shook her head, "No! I was a shot girl, and so was my friend D– Donna. A lot of guys hung out there who are 'big deals.'" She used air quotes. "D'you know what I mean?" Felix wasn't sure he knew what she meant, and he desperately wanted to. He just nodded, and she continued. "I worked there for almost a year and started dating this guy. He was super nice at first, and a cool guy, you know? He had some 'Big Deal' buddies."

"Wait, like the Mafia? Drug dealers?" Felix leaned back slightly, anxious for her to get to the point. His stomach was scrunched up with worry at how her story was going to unfold.

"Maybe? I dunno. I didn't ask. I was dumb about it. Maybe I should have found out." She licked her lips and took a deep breath. "So not only was there something flirty going on between Billy and my girlfriend, but this boyfriend of mine turned out to be a real asshole. I had an app business of my own and started to make some really good money. He wanted it. He wanted me to invest in his side business but wouldn't tell me what it was." Natalie's face grew indignant, her fear slipping into anger.

Felix watched her mouth and her sparking green eyes and gave her a little more room on the couch. "Was it drugs? You can tell me."

She scoffed. "No! Geez, it isn't always drugs. I mean, Billy might have been on drugs. Things between us didn't go that far for me to know for certain. When I wouldn't loan him fifty thousand dollars, his actions made me end things with him. Or, I'd tried. We were on a break, at least. That is when I moved out."

"Fifty thousand dollars!" Felix's voice raised several notches. "You have that kind of money?" The woman before him unfurled from her spot on the couch to stretch her back, and a tiny grin formed on her lips.

"You'd be surprised how lucrative feet are." She lost her scared look, and suddenly, the flirtatious Natalie from last night was before him. He sat there dumbly, trying to process what she'd said.

Felix never understood foot fetishes, and now the woman he liked confessed she sold pictures of her feet? Or did she– do things – with her feet? "Do you, err, do things?" He didn't know how to finish the sentence. Was this a weird new *Pretty Woman* situation, but with feet?

She bubbled a tense laugh and the burnt sugar fragrance caressed his face when she leaned towards him. "No! No, not that I wouldn't…taking pictures of my feet is no biggie. I created an app that users sign up for, and another company invested in it. It really took off in the first six months. I've made quite a bit of money. A lot."

Felix was nodding and stood up, moving to the kitchen to get a drink from the small fridge.

"So, now we have established I am neither a stripper nor a foot geisha. Are you still 'Team Natalie'?"

"Yes. I wish you weren't so worried to tell me this stuff. This is… well, it isn't a big deal, *Sweetling*." Felix dramaticized the endearment to lighten the mood, but Natalie's face was downcast.

"None of that was my secret." She grimaced, and Felix took a deep breath, feeling really nervous now. *Who was this girl?*

CHAPTER 17

Niagara

Natalie grabbed a glass from the kitchen area and poured a glug of whisky from a nearly full bottle sitting on the counter. "Yes, I kept my work and the big house a secret, but the big deal is Billy. I'd moved out of his apartment and was staying with a friend. My friend Do– Donna who was flirty with him, always had a thing for him, like I said. She went to pay him a visit, console him or something."

Felix sat straighter, thunking the beverage down on a side table. "That is –"

Natalie pressed her fingers to his lips before he could dress down this bitch of a friend. "He raped her." Natalie stopped, watching his face for a reaction.

They sat on the couch facing each other, neither one looking away. She saw horror, anger, pain, and confusion all ripple through his beautiful eyes. It was the better response. "She didn't want to tell me because she thought it was her fault. She'd gone over there to sniff around; she'd always liked him, but she and I were close, as close as work buddies could be, I guess, like you and Maisie. It came out a week or two after the fact. She never went to the police."

Felix leaned towards her, taking her arm and whispering, "but you could have reported it then..."

The blonde shook her head sadly. "He'd been harassing her, stalking me, still trying to get me to 'invest' and threatening me with his 'friends' if I didn't help him out. I'd had to leave my job because it got really scary having him and his pals showing up, disrupting my work."

Felix patted her hand absently as she spoke.

"When I finally found out he'd attacked Do-Dori." She shakes herself and looks at him warily before continuing, "Okay, her name wasn't Donna. I was trying to hide her from you by changing her name. Dori. When I finally found out, I wanted her to go to the police. She begged me not to say anything. She was scared of him, ashamed she'd flirted with him, and felt she deserved the attack." Felix began to open his mouth to argue, and Natalie almost loved him for it.

"No. Please, let me get this out. There is more."

His mouth snapped shut, and he sat back, resigned.

"I got her to agree that we would go together to confront him and get him to fuck on off for good, or we would go to the police. It was a way for both of us to get closure and get rid of this asshole.

He became really irate, and we were foolish to go to his place without any kind of protection. He was an evil person, and I was an idiot to let him sweep me off my feet."

Felix took her hands in his. "Are you in danger now?"

Her green eyes turned darker and filled with tears. "I don't know if his people would bother looking for me, but they did reach out to Dori, asking questions about me."

Felix sat up straighter and squeezed her hands.

"I will protect you."

She felt a chuckle rise in her throat as this sweet man looked so fierce and earnest. He was making promises he was not equipped to carry out, but she appreciated his intent. "You don't have to worry about him coming after me." Natalie's voice was stronger.

Felix moved to where she huddled against the corner of the couch. "Well, I'm going to worry about it. I'm going to worry about anyone who's going to do anything but make your day better, and this Billy guy sounds dangerous".

"Yeah, well, we don't have to worry about him."

Felix studied her face. She studied him. He looked worried and so angry. She had to reassure him, so she added one word: "Now."

"Now?" Felix repeated her words slowly, barely comprehending. "What do you mean, '*We*

don't have to worry about him now'?"

"Just that we don't have to worry about him anymore." Felix stared, considering, and she struggled not to look away. As she met his eyes, her stomach tensed in desire and also fear. His prince in shining armor persona was pretty sexy. What if Felix left her now? What if when he hears this truth, it is too much, and he goes? She couldn't blame him, of course, but she hoped this beautiful boy in front of her would stay.

"How certain are you that he is not going to come after you and hurt you?"

Natalie sighed, kept her eyes on his and said, "Well, pretty certain."

Felix didn't move and kept his eyes on hers. She wanted him to get it, but he wasn't sure what 'it' was. He put his big, warm hands on her shoulders and distracted himself with the warmth of her skin. Natalie imagined him running them down the rest of her body. "Natalie, when you say we don't have to worry about him anymore, and you say that you are certain...."

"I mean that he's dead." Her voice caught in her throat. She hadn't admitted this to anyone. No one but Dori, and she was there. "He is dead and he's not going to bother me anymore."

"Oh my God. Did you kill him?" Felix moved back slightly but didn't release her hands.

"I didn't say that. I just said that– I know that he's dead."

He studied Natalie a little bit longer in

silence. He'd never met a girl like this before, and he didn't know what to say to all of this. He said only, "Okay."

Felix squeezed her hands, threading his fingers through hers, and nodded gently. Natalie's throat felt choked with breath, and she could not get air in or out. She was going to start wheezing like an asthmatic, which only happens during the Spring allergy season, but this felt very similar. She felt a little swirly in her mind and wondered if she was actually going to faint like a goddamn book girl.

Felix pulled her close and wrapped his arms around her, holding tight. She sagged against him, though she probably should run. No one needed to be involved in her sordid past. Her mind flitted to his strong arms, she was kind of proud of his arms. It's obvious he had, in fact, been working out. She admired the fact he seemed to be focused on being his best. It looked good on him. And he was a good worker, kind, funny, and well-read. She wondered where his books were…she suddenly wanted to see his nightstand.

"Are you certain that no one else is going to come after you? From that part of your life?"

Natalie met his eyes and replied, "Dead sure."

They both took a deep breath, sitting in silence.

She told him that the two women had gone to his loft on Wacker Drive. The confrontation was volatile and dangerous as they stood in his loft foyer. Bill had reached for what Natalie thought was a weapon. When he was turned away from them, she reacted. She pushed him.

The three of them stood at the top of a twisting open staircase, and with his hands essentially in a pocket, he couldn't stop the fall or grab the railing. The two women watched Billy fall down the stairs in a horrific end-over-end tumble to the bottom. He lay face down and motionless on the landing, blood pooling around his head. The two women turned and fled through the front door. They chose to both run and plead ignorance if anyone asked what they knew about his death.

"Oh my God, Natalie!" He petted her as his mind raced with the information. Was the woman he adored a murderer? Was she still in danger? Was she being honest? Felix remembered the text that started this waterfall of revelations from the beautiful, tragic blonde in front of him. "But what was the text, then?" He watched fear flitter across her eyes.

"I dunno. I mean, Billy wasn't connected, really, I think he was all talk. But. Someone reached out, and it scared me again. No one knows I'm here. I used the name Nancy at the club, even with Billy. It was a nickname, a cover, kind of. You know, that street life."

Felix didn't know, but he couldn't admit he was a completely sheltered mama's boy in the middle of Natalie's turmoil. He just nodded like a dipshit.

The nodding and keeping his stupid mouth shut worked because she leaned into him then. He thought she was moving to kiss him, so he leaned in for the kiss. She reared back, green eyes wide and startled. Nope, wrong signal.

But then, just as quickly, her face changed again. She thought to herself, with all this other fuckery, why not? She smiled a genuine, lopsided smile at the good guy in front of her, the nice guy who knew all her secrets and only seemed to want her more. Natalie leaned a little closer, leaving only inches between them. Their eyes locked, and sparks flew, and she said, "Okay, then." Her eyes fluttered shut as she pursed her swollen lips and leaned forward.

Felix cupped her face in his hands, and when their lips met, he was so relieved he wanted to cry like a baby. He hadn't realized how much stress his body held, aching to touch this girl. Their lips slid and moved together, slightly apart, back together, and she did a tiny chuckle against his lips. "If you are laughing, I must be doing it wrong?" He whispered.

She laughed again, nuzzling her face against his neck where the collar of his shirt parted. "It is so nice."

"Nice? I thought girls hated that." He tried to look at her, but her face was planted against his neck.

"Girls might not like nice guys, but women

do. I do. I like you, Felix. I have for a while." Her lips found his again, and they spent the rest of their lives sitting on the couch, kissing, as the daylight sunk into darkness.

Okay, not the rest of their lives, that is a bit dramatic, but it was a long, long while.

CHAPTER 18

Don't Bother to Knock

The lunch rush was almost over, and Rose McCall could not breathe. She kept trying and felt faint. The room swam, the din of diners and staff and dishes and the smells of food all swarmed her senses at once. As the seconds ticked by, the weight on her chest didn't let up. The panic was starting to claw at her from the inside. She could feel it: the sensation of drowning, the fear that if she didn't get help soon, it might be too late. She wanted to scream, but the words got caught in her throat.

Maisie hovered nearby, fear on her sweet young features. "Rose? Are you…" She stopped, eyes growing wider as this iconic woman seemed to age in seconds. "I'm calling 911!"

Rose nodded when her breath eased up. "I'm sick, Maisie," Rose finally admitted, her voice barely above a whisper. The confession was raw, and it surprised even her. At that moment, with the girls' steady presence beside her, she couldn't keep up the act any longer. "Please call Felix, let him know I'm going to the hospital."

Maisie didn't say anything at first. She

simply squeezed Rose's shoulder and nodded, her face full of empathy. The dispatcher on the phone was asking questions Maisie struggled to answer. She kept talking to Rose, reassuring her as she sank to the floor, gasping for breath. "You don't have to be scared. I'm here, okay? We'll get you through this. No one's going to make a big deal out of it. I promise."

Rose closed her eyes and let out a shaky breath. Maybe it wasn't so bad to admit she needed help. Maybe, just maybe, it was okay to be human.

As Maisie spoke to the dispatcher, and then the paramedics, Rose felt a pang of anxiety. She couldn't shake the thought of what would happen when everyone found out. She knew, deep down, that her family would be there for her. Felix would be there, no matter what. Maisie, was here, and Natalie, too. And for the first time since her husband Tom died, Rose didn't feel quite so alone. She wondered if she would see Tom soon. Would he like her hair? Would he call her Rose?

***

Another text, just like the first lit up Natalie's phone later that night. She and Felix had kissed until they were bruised and exhausted. They dozed off in between conversations about their entire childhood and adult life, likes, dislikes, what food had to be in the fridge, and what was absolutely not allowed. She felt a flare of anger at the text. It felt better than the fear from the other night.

ZIDLER: Fuck off

She moved to turn her phone off and snuggle back into Felix. His hand on her wrist stopped her.

"Don't you think you should look into this?"

She fought the urge to glare at him. It was a good idea. She didn't like it. "No. Haven't you heard the phrase, 'Let sleeping dogs lie?'"

Felix chuckled and retorted, "Chaucer. Good one. This is your life, though. Your safety. Someone is fucking with you, and you don't want to find out who it is?"

Natalie's mouth hung open. "That's where it came from? Chaucer? I had no idea."

"Well, if obscure facts turn you on, I am a wellspring, but first, we need to sort this out. Together. I am Team Natalie, and you don't have to do this alone." He pulled her to him and squeezed, feeling her physically relax. They sat on the lumpy couch, legs intertwined, talking about options for over an hour. It felt so good to be able to talk about her secret and have a partner to help with the scary possibilities. Then, this beautiful man said the magic words.

"I could Google him."

Her mouth closed with a small snap, and she pulled her legs up to her chest, wrapping her arms around them. To avoid responding, she pulled a cold slice of Greenhouse pizza from the box on his coffee table. She made a performance of chewing. An olive fell off, plopping on her chest. Their eyes met, and he wiggled his eyebrows. Her eyebrows invited him to try, and he leaped to slurp the offending olive into his mouth. Felix wasn't cool or suave. The olive escaped his lips and landed on the carpet. He plucked it up with his long fingers, "five-minute rule." She watched the now hairy olive disappear into his lips. Laughter barked out of her pale lips, and he joined her.

"I've been afraid to Google, worried they could find me that way."

"What was his name? Surely it was in the news? What exactly happened?" His questions came rapid fire, and she took a few moments to reply.

"I haven't seen him in the news. His name was Bill Penz. Billy. And I figured his friends, if he had them, covered it up." She finished the pizza, watching Felix think. Maybe he would have a solution. She hoped he would.

He typed into his phone, clicking and clucking over whatever was there. "Well, he doesn't have any social media." Natalie nodded, but Felix was staring at his phone. He looked up with a roguish grin, "But then again, neither do you, my *Sweetling*."

She shrugged one shoulder. "The club set up media for us and used our pictures. If you looked at their feed, you'd see me. I was too busy to bother with social media. I just lived."

"I don't see Bill Penz anywhere. Not in the news, or on social media. No LinkedIn–" His words cut off as Natalie wailed with heaving sounds he finally clocked as laughter.

"No one has LinkedIn in the club scene, Felix! Are you kidding me?"

Felix tried to look annoyed, but inside, he felt downright dumb. Of course, the clubbers wouldn't be on LinkedIn. He was just trying to cross all of their t's. Christ Jesus. She was laughing at him so hard. He didn't like it at all. He was going to tell her until his phone buzzed, and it was a text from Maisie.

MOUTHY MAISIE: WHere are you? Rose ambo to hosp meet her
FELIX THE GREAT: What
MOUTHY MAISIE: Go to Porterer at Roosevelllltewt

He stood up fast, and Natalie swallowed her ongoing laughter. She rose when he did, reaching for his arm. "What is it?"

He tried to answer, but his lips felt numb. He struggled and replied, "My Mom is in the ER." Natalie's eyes rounded in alarm, and she looked around them.

"Uh, let's go. Which ER? Is she sick?" They clumsily gathered phones and jackets, and she followed him from the apartment to where he'd parked his car earlier that day.

"I don't know. I– Maisie just called, and... she collapsed at work and is being taken to Roosevelt ER."

"Why is Maisie calling you?"

Felix slid into the driver's seat and looked at Natalie askance. "They were at work."

Natalie looked puzzled and asked, "Who is your Mom?"

Felix knew they were subtle about their Mother-son relationship, but he thought everyone knew. "Rose is my mom."

The flabbergasted look on Natalie's face would have entertained him if he had not been so focused on getting to the hospital. He backed jerkily out of the parallel spot on Lincolnway and headed to Roosevelt. Natalie seemed more upset by this news than he could justify. Tears once again filled her eyes, and she worried the strap of her bag between her fingers as he drove.

"I - I didn't know." She looked at him fearfully, "Is she worse?"

At the next stoplight, he turned squarely to meet her inquisitive face. "What do you mean, 'Is she worse?' What do I not know?" Natalie looked dark then, a shuttering of her features that raised his alarm bells. "Natalie?" His voice sounded harsh in his own ears, but she was keeping something from him. Something about his mother.

"I didn't say that. I don't know." The light changed, and she pointed to the green orb. He hit the gas, and they rode in silence for several minutes.

"Did she tell you something?"

"No, I... she had an episode and I helped her. She asked me not to tell anyone."

"She is my mother, Natalie!" He was pissed. The muscles in his neck and shoulders twisted up with tension. All the stress of the day and now this text from Maisie it was all too much. His emotions boiled over and the resulting blowup landed in Natalie's lap.

"I didn't know that, Felix." Her voice sounded calm but strained. "She asked me to keep it between us. I thought I was being discreet about a private matter." She faced forward as he drove the rest of the way to the ER. He pulled in, and when she moved to get out of the car, he shook his head.

"No. Please do not come with me. Call an Uber or something." Natalie's mouth fell open in surprise, and her heart dropped into her chest. Felix turned on her, tears in his eyes. "How dare you know my mother is sick and keep it a secret?" He turned away again, striding to the emergency room doors.

Worry for Rose and concern for Felix clouded Natalie's judgment. Instead of giving him space, she jogged after him through the parking lot. Her voice burst out of her chest, sounding plaintive and desperate. "She asked me to, and I didn't know, Felix. I am coming with you. I am worried about her too; I care about Rose." She wiped hair out of her face, confused at his reaction, uncertain how to handle all the emotions of this day.

Felix ignored her, hustling through the sliding doors to the reception desk. Natalie could hear the hubbub of medical teams, bored patients, and the Chicago news on the television. Her brain and nerves were on fire as she worried about Rose and feared Felix's anger. Tears pricked her eyes, and she fiddled with her purse strap and her rumpled hair as she anxiously waited for them to be sent back to see Rose.

At last, a nurse or an aide or whoever ushered them towards a pair of mechanical doors, but Felix stopped Natalie with his hand against her chest. "No. You go." He turned away from her, and the confused nurse shrugged and followed him, leaving Natalie standing tearfully in the ER lobby. After a few moments, she just sat back down to wait with her heart in her throat.

CHAPTER 19

The Crowening

"Oh, Darrrrrrling! I am so glad you are here." Felix cleared the curtain to find Rose behind it, flowing blonde hair in a long wig, cell phone in her manicured hand.

"Mom!"

"Be a good boy and get Sheila out of my bag, won't you?" His mother's voice had always been smoky and dramatic, but Felix found the affectations she had embraced post-Schitt's Creek show a bit annoying. Instead of obeying, he stood dumbly beside the bed, looking bewildered. His mother however, appeared to be holding court quite nicely in ER exam room four. She had a drink in a styrofoam cup on the side table, a blanket that felt warm to the touch, and her cell phone held tightly in one of her bejeweled hands. She avoided his gaze, tapping the phone screen with her free hand.

"Mom." *Tap. tap.*

"Mmm?" *Taptaptaptappity–*

"MOM. What is going on here? Are you okay?"

She dragged her gaze from the phone and met his eyes furtively before replying.

"My daaaaarling boy. You may not have been top of your class, but suuurrrely you see where we are." She looked away as someone medical flitted in and back out again with a professionally plastic smile to both of them.

"Well, no, of course not, but Natalie said–"

His mother's dark eyes turned fierce. "What did Natalie say? She swore she could keep a secret."

Felix shifted to sit beside her on the bed, taking her hand still holding the phone and squeezed gently, phone and all. She'd have to be buried with the damn thing. She was like a teenager about it. Social media, her fashion Instagram, all of it so silly.

"She didn't tell me anything, what– why would she know about... whatever this is," he gestured to the room, his mother in the narrow bed somehow looking frail and queenly at the same time, "before I do? I am your son, for Christ's sake!"

Rose dropped her phone to the bed and clasped his hand with her IV hand. She caressed his ruddy cheek with her free hand. "Yes darling, but you worry. She's a peach and happened to be in the right place at the wrong time. I had to trust her to keep my secret."

"What secret? You aren't dying, right?" He looked wildly around for any indication of her imminent demise. She looked the same as always, the long waves of her blonde wig staticky against the bed pillow. She was maybe paler? Or wearing less makeup? Her colorful jewelry always took center stage...was she looking this ill before, and he'd fucking missed it?

"Pshaw, everyone is dying, dear boy. " Her face was serious. He felt tears spring up behind his eyes, and his throat tightened. "I might die very soon, if you don't do as I asked."

"What?" Felix felt confused, scared and irritated by her dramatic non-answers.

"Get Shelia out of my bag. Glinda is too much for this situation." She gestured to her oversized turquoise tote bag, and understanding dawned on him. Shelia. Glinda. Her wigs. She wanted a different wig from her bag. *A friggin costume change in the ER?* His mother was precious, but this was off the charts. He opened his mouth to tell her so, and she gasped a bit, reaching for the drink cup. He helped her and then hurried around the narrow bed to retrieve the wig.

"Oh, my gawd. Sheila is so much better suited to this moment. Thank you, Felix." Rose finger-combed the shorter brunette shag style and slipped it over the wig cap that covered her real hair, which was thinner and greyer than he remembered. *When had his mother gotten old?* Rose handed him the ziplock bag and the discarded wig cradled in a hairnet. He dropped the big blonde monstrosity into her bag and turned back to her.

He was going to get stern with her about

fessing up to her health issues when a doctor and the nurse from earlier entered. They spoke back and forth about her symptoms, how long she'd had them, why a family doctor hadn't seen her, and what tests they would run next. Felix was going to ask a few questions of his own when his mother took over the room. Rose sat up as straight as she could in the awkward hospital cot. She tossed her shorter hair and applied lipstick, which she'd somehow stashed in a pocket.

She spoke as if to a crowd of royal subjects. "Now listen. I am not interested in any of that business. I am not here to pay for your kid's college fund, Ms. Doctor." She gestured wanly to the doctor with this comment. "I am old as hell, my body is tired, and we will just let this slide by. Do you understand?" She eyed Felix, whose voice suddenly boomed through the tiny room.

"No, we will not, Mom!" Felix couldn't get close to her because the medical team was in the way, but he raised his voice and wished it sounded stronger. "You listen to them and get whatever care you need for whatever this is." He wiped his clammy hands on his jeans and faced the previously smiling nurse, "What did you say this is?"

The nurse looked to the doctor, who nodded at Felix's outburst and directed her words to Rose in the bed. "This is your son? Are you comfortable discussing your medical details with him?"

Rose made a dismissive gesture and nodded

'Yes.'

The doctor turned to Felix and said, "From our brief information gathering, it looks like your mother is experiencing lung failure. She may have acute exacerbation from emphysema that has been untreated for some time. We have a battery of tests we could run, and we can treat some symptoms, abating these types of episodes. According to the information she shared today, several underlying factors may complicate the situation. Our initial physical exam brought up several concerns that she is not interested in discussing. Again, we cannot learn more details without running the tests."

Felix sat heavily on the edge of the bed, almost missing it. He took a breath and looked at his mother. Her gaze was not defiant now. She looked sad, and maybe scared.

Rose McCall was always larger than life, and he realized he'd expected her to always play her role. He was not ready to lose her. His mind reeled as he stared at his mother.

"Are you dying?" She reached for his hand again.

"Like I was saying before, aren't we all, Darling?" The delivery was different this time, though; it was more serious. Felix lunged for his mother like a small boy, taking her into his arms. Tears began to dampen his t-shirt as they both held on to each other and wept.

A soft cough from the foot of the bed

reminded them there was an audience. The nurse checked charts and futzed with dials. The doctor spoke softly to them both. "We'll let you two talk awhile, and check in with you on the testing in a few minutes."

Neither mother nor son looked up as the curtain slid across the entryway, leaving them with their feelings.

CHAPTER 20

Clash By Night

Natalie sat in the far corner of the waiting room, nursing a cold cup of coffee that is thin enough to be classified as tea. Her eyes darted to the window at every passing shadow. The weight of her worn hoodie hides her face, and her fingers fidget nervously on the table. How long will Felix be? She had to make it right between them. She had to.

She also wanted to know about Rose, how she was doing and would she be mad that Felix knew she was…what? What was Rose doing? Just being sick, or was she dying?

The texts kept making her phone vibrate, and each line squeezed the heart in her chest. Everything was falling apart.

UNKNOWN CALLER: Hi Nancy

Natalie froze, the name landing like a hammer. Slowly, she raises the phone, her eyes wary and guarded. She looks around the waiting room, hoping he isn't here. Where was Felix? Was Rose even alive? Is that why he hadn't come back yet? Did he know she was waiting, that she cared so much about both of them? Her phone buzzed again.

UNKNOWN CALLER: or is it Natalie?
ZIDLER: Who is this
UNKNOWN CALLER: You know
ZIDLER: I thought you were gone
UNKNOWN CALLER: I know. I found out a lot recently. It took me long enough, huh?
ZIDLER: WHat do you wnat? I didnt go to the police about what you did
UNKNOWN CALLER: So generous, just tried to kill me. I didn't go to cops either sweetheart.
ZIDLER: What do you want Billy
UNKNOWN CALLER: Call and talk

She thinks about how to respond for so long her whirling brain almost blocks out the buzz of the phone in her hand. She answers, looking around again to see if he is somehow there, watching her. A shiver runs up her spine, but she only sees a young couple with a baby, a middle-aged man, and the staff milling about the emergency room.

He found her, but he wasn't here.

He is not here. She tries to take a deep breath, failing. She presses her palm into her chest to make herself calm down. She looks at the main door to the ER rooms, anxiously hoping Felix will walk back out the doors with good news and a smile for her.

Instead, Billy's voice is in her ear, turning her stomach with apprehension.

"I quit the booze. I'm in AA. Twelve steps, you know? I'm... I'm on the ninth. Making amends."

"Amends? You think an apology can fix– "

"No. I don't think it'll fix anything. But I need to say it. For me." Natalie snorts despite her fear. She hears him shift papers on the phone. "For you, if you'll let me." Natalie's jaw tightens, her hands trembling slightly as she clenches the paper coffee cup, now cold. The woman with the baby rifles through a diaper bag for something.

Everyone here has their own troubles, but no one knows Natalie's real story. No one but Felix, and he hates her now. She tries to reign in her wild thoughts to the voice in her ear. "Did you hunt me down just to say 'sorry'? You've got some nerve."

"I didn't hunt you down. I called in a favor."

"I'll bet. From The Boys."

"Yeah. They wanted to...do something about our... situation, you know. I said not to make a move. I just couldn't leave things the way they were." He stops talking, and she can hear him breathing. Even his breathing used to turn her on, two years ago, when she was dumb. So much has changed since then, and he could ruin it all for her in so many ways.

She realizes he is still talking and tries to keep fear in check.

"You didn't deserve— "

Her fear turned to outrage. She spit out the words, "You don't get to decide what I deserve!"

"You're right. I don't. And I need to own up to what I did. I was a mess back then... drunk, angry, out of control. I took it out on you. I hurt you in ways I can't even imagine."

"You raped Dori."

"That was– "

"You raped her."

"Okay." His voice was low and tight. All of the personal growth she'd done since leaving, since making her own money with the app, it all slid away when his voice was in her ear. She was once again the insecure girl, scrabbling for the scraps of his attention.

"I will never forgive you." Her voice shook, and she was embarrassed he could likely hear it. The people in the waiting room were watching her with concern now. She'd been too loud just then. She is too much. She steps towards the hospital doors and stands just outside, away from the bored Valet sitting on a folding chair. Billy kept talking in her ear, back from the dead to ruin her life.

"I know. And I'm not asking for forgiveness. I just... I'm sorry, Nancy. For everything." Silence hangs between them, heavy and unspoken. Natalie shifts the phone to her other ear, her expression unreadable.

"You don't get a gold star for saying you are sorry."

"I know."

"You showing up on my phone—it's not just about you being sorry. It's a reminder. Of everything I've been trying to leave behind."

"I didn't mean to drag you back to Chicago."

"But you are."

"I'm sorry. If there's anything I can do to make it right, I'll do it. I'm serious, Nance."

"Maybe just... leave me alone." She listens for a moment to the silence between them – relieved that he is not dead, that she is not a murderer, and that this might be over. "Have you talked to Dori?"

"She is on my list. That call is harder."

"I'll bet it is. You are a fucking horrible person."

"She isn't blameless..."

"Fuck you. A woman can throw themselves naked at a man, and if she says 'No' there is no other word that matters."

He is silent, and she can imagine him at the other end of the line, getting angry and frustrated because he knows he is in the wrong. He'd be raking his hands through the crewcut, pacing. It is no longer her job to cater to his goddamn feelings, so she finishes her statement. "You apologize to her, and offer to do whatever she wants to make it right. I still think she should have gone straight to the police."

She can barely hear his one-word reply. "Okay."

"I'm hanging up now. I never want to see you

or talk to you again, and if I do, I will go to the police and tell them everything."

"I'm gone, Girl." The phone clicks, and all that is left are his text messages.

Natalie feels shaky with relief and her legs are unsteady. She sinks onto the brick planter edge, her thumb hovering over the trashcan icon. With one tap, the scary conversation disappears like the brunette once known as 'Nancy'.

The blonde with dark roots sits for a long time, taking deep breaths at last. She sends a text and waits only fifteen minutes before the cavalry arrives.

"Hey, Doll!" The pink-haired girl with a big smile rolled down the passenger side window, and ska music poured out of the beat-up little blue car. "Need a ride?" Natalie grinned weakly and slid into the seat next to her friend.

"Thanks, Maisie."

"Ohmygawd don't. I'm yours." As her friend navigated the parking lot, Natalie felt the tears threaten to flow any moment. She pressed her hands to her face.

"Can we get some food? I have a story to tell you."

CHAPTER 21

We're Not Married

Somehow, Natalie got her proverbial shit together to show up for the dinner shift the next day. The TITS group chat was lively and busy with updates on Rose's hospital stay and the usual restaurant chatter about logistics and gossip. Felix did not reply to any of it, and everyone noticed the absolute radio silence from him.

Several regulars asked about Rose, and Natalie figured the news wouldn't have to travel far if she'd left here in an ambulance just yesterday. She put them off gently and did her best to smile for her tables, help her colleagues, and not acknowledge the ache that Felix wasn't there and hadn't responded to her texts.

To be fair, he hadn't replied to any of them, but Natalie felt his silence deeply.

"Whatcha thinking about?" Natalie's head snapped up at Tom's smoky voice. She was flustered to see him and swayed backwards as if pushed. He snapped one of his big muscled arms to catch her, "Whoa! You okay?"

She steadied herself and nodded. "Hi. Yeah,

it has been a lot the past few days. You heard about Rose?"

He nodded. "How is she?"

Natalie shook her head slowly, scanning the dining room to see if her tables needed her. They didn't. "I don't know. She's still in the hospital."

"Of course, else she'd be here, yeah?" His dumb face was such a sweet sight, worrying about her and Rose. Thor. She hadn't returned his calls lately and felt a twinge of guilt.

"I'm sorry I didn't call you back."

He wrapped an arm all the way around her shoulders, drawing her into his warmth. He smelled faintly like his house, cheap apple and something manly, some kind of cologne he wore too heavily. "No worries. We aren't married, right?"

He tried to mock her, looking around comically as if to make certain they were not, in fact, married. Natalie didn't laugh, but she sank down onto the barstool beside him. Jessica and Cheyanne were futzing behind the bar, and without a word, Jessica placed a glass of fizzing cola in front of Natalie. She also slid a draft beer in front of Tom, the foam still fresh.

"How are you doing, kid?" Jessica could be talking to either of them, but her eyes were on Natalie, and they were concerned.

"Okay. Have you heard anything?"

Jessica sighed, shaking her head. "No... I am so worried."

Tom sipped his beer, and his eyes drifted to the TV mounted in the corner.

"You really don't know anything? I figured you are banging the owner's son, you'd know the deets."

Natalie coughed, wiped the spilled soda, and met Jessica's eyes with her own. "I'm not... banging...him."

"So sorry, my Queen, I was crude...I meant making sweet love."

Natalie looked at Tom, who acted as if his life suddenly depended on whatever was on the TV screen.

"No, it's not like that. We don't uh do that."

Jessica stopped leering at her and crossed her arms in disbelief. "You mean that poor dude has been pining for weeks, and you haven't done the deed?"

Tom drained his beer, dropped a twenty on the bar, and said, "Good luck with that, Gorgeous." He turned and strolled away from both of them.

"Felix and I are friends. Or we were." She craned her neck around the corner to survey her tables. One group was sitting stiffly, and she realized they were probably ready for a check. She slid off the barstool to do her job.

Several minutes later, Natalie was at the end of the bar and Jessica came to take her order. As she poured cocktails and beer, Natalie asked the question that burned since yesterday. "Does everyone here but me know Felix is Rose's son?"

Jessica looked serious for a moment. "You didn't?"

"No! Why?"

Jessica served another guest and then replied, "We thought that was why you guys hung out?"

Natalie choked on her offense. Jessica kept her eyes on Natalie's even as she delivered a glass of wine to a new bar patron. "What? You thought I was a gold digger or something?"

"We did. At first, I mean, we know you now." Jessica's face reflected concern at Natalie's obvious hurt. "But we like you. We all do."

Natalie thought she'd had them all in hand, but really, they had brought her into the inner circle because they actually liked her. She had been pegged as a gold digger, but as the walls came down, real friendships had bloomed. She felt the tears and couldn't put down the tray of drinks, as Jessica had already set more glasses down for other orders.

Jessica gasped at Natalie's wet cheeks, leaning deftly over the bar with a napkin to pat them dry. "I'm sorry."

"No, it's okay. I can understand."

The conversation ended as the dinner crowd flowed. Natalie's heart was heavy. On one hand, she had Cheyenne, Jessica and Maisie as good friends. On the other hand, she may have lost the friendship... and whatever else was there, with Felix. She cared so much for Rose, and she couldn't even get an update since she was *persona non grata* there right now. Nothing would work out until she could look at Felix, talk to him, and explain again.

Almost as if she summoned him, Felix's face appeared at the hostess stand, and the TITS gang instantly swarmed him. Natalie hung back, knowing the restaurant was no place for the conversation they needed to have.

After the initial swarm dissipated, Felix looked around and found her, gesturing for her to come to him. She went willingly with her heart in her mouth. Has Rose explained it to him? Was he still angry? Natalie almost skipped to him, eager to hear that Rose was better, maybe even home already. When her hopeful face was close enough to his, she saw he was serious and closed off to her. He didn't smile or reach for her. All was not forgiven. She stopped short, waiting before him for a word, for anything.

"Rose would like you to visit her tomorrow morning. At the hospital."

Natalie opened her mouth to ask all of her questions, but he dismissed her with a sharp turn of his body and he exited through the front doors.

Natalie's heart broke in her chest. What the hell? What were all these big emotions in a twenty-four-hour period? Did she have feelings for the man leaving her behind? She hadn't even admitted it to herself; how could he know? They'd had such a unique, exhausting afternoon on his couch, but they hadn't really talked about anything but her problems. She'd become a shit friend and a shit employee in a moment. Life was too much this week. Too much pain, too much honesty, too much emotion.

If Felix knew she wanted him, would it help this misunderstanding between them? She plunged through the doors, hoping the gang would look after her tables.

"Felix!" He must have parked right outside the door, because he was already gone.

CHAPTER 22

How to Marry a Millionaire

"Rose?" Natalie whispered, afraid to wake the frail-looking woman resting with her eyes closed. She lay back on white hospital pillows, but was wearing a colorful, silky robe. Her pale, gnarled hands lay unmoving on top of a crazy quilt that must have been brought from home. It looked odd in the stark hospital room. Natalie saw the IV in Roses' hand and the stand with two bags hanging there. There were four floral arrangements in a variety of sizes and colors lining the window of the room. What appeared to be an untouched meal tray lay on the side table, next to a tube of lipstick and a cell phone.

"Deplorable, isn't it?" Natalie started at the sudden sound, then smiled at the beloved drawn out words, *"deploooraaable, isn't it?"*

She moved to the bed then, grasping Rose's available hand in both of hers. "Rose. Are you okay?"

The older woman released her hand to brush the brunette bob away from her red lipsticked lips. "I find it preposterous that people keep inquiring about my health when I am so obviously in a hospital. I question our local school system's efficacy." Every word spoken tautly, with extra vowels and her unique inflection. Or, with Catherine O'Hara's Shitt's Creek inflections, anyway.

"We are all so worried."

"Well, you all should stop that. It is a waste of this beautiful life." Rose pulled Natalie close enough she had to sit on the bed. It was awkward, but there wasn't anywhere she'd rather be at the moment. Rose breathed shallowly, and Natalie took in the buttons and remote controls, wondering if she needed to summon help. Rose seemed to calm down, and they just looked at each other for a while. The hiss and beep of whatever Rose was attached to was the only sound for several moments.

"You look good, of course."

Rose rolled her shoulder to dismiss the compliment, but Natalie saw pleasure on her face. "You look terrible, Darling." Rose tried to look stern, reaching for Natalie's face. Natalie leaned forward to help the woman reach her. Rose's hand was cool against her cheek, and smelled vaguely of lilac. "Do not break my son's heart, dear girl."

Natalie pulled back, startled. "We are just– "

"He is in love with you."

Natalie's mouth dropped open, and she sat up, spinning once again. "We are..." She stopped, stuck. What are they? They'd shared deeply, kissed passionately, and she had to admit she had growing feelings for this would-be knight in shining armor.

"You know I speak the truth. You aren't a dumb blonde no matter how you act. Never kid a kidder."

"He has been very good to me."

"Ah. So you do not feel the same." Rose looked as if she had expected this. Natalie racked her brain for words, but they wouldn't come. "You could do worse than Felix McCall. He will inherit Trailside, has two degrees and graduated top of his class. He has a heart of gold."

"Yes…"

"And he loves his mother, you know that can go either way, but I think I am a catch as a mother-in-law, don't you?"

"Rose, the thing is…"

"Natalie, the thing is… I've watched Felix come alive since you walked into Trailside. The customers love you, the staff loves you, and I'd bet my right tit Felix loves you too."

Natalie had heard enough. She jumped up from the bed, standing over Rose to grab control of this terrible conversation. "You don't understand. Felix doesn't feel that way anymore. He knows I knew you were sick and he is furious at me."

"Oh, that? Don't be silly. You know men have their little tirades, and they always come home. I've never seen my son so smitten as he is with you. He'll get over it."

Natalie crossed her arms and turned from Rose's overconfident face. Her voice was low and sad as she spoke. "No, he wouldn't speak to me except to share your message to come today. I don't know what to do to change his mind."

She heard Rose sigh deeply which changed to a racking cough. Natalie whirled around and looked on with alarm. "Do I need to call someone?"

Rose shook her head, coughed, wheezed, and dabbed her eyes with a cloth handkerchief. The episode lasted minutes but felt like hours. Something beeped on the monitors, and an alarm sounded, bringing nurses quickly into the room.

Vitals were taken and Rose recovered, waving everyone but Natalie out of the room. She looked exhausted. Natalie tried to put a bright smile on her face to cheer the older woman.

"Knock that shit off. Do not try to placate me. This is bad. I don't need anyone grinning maniacally at me. I am dying. I am not a fool." Rose rasped.

"Of course. They cannot do anything for you? To help?" Natalie stood shifting from foot to foot beside Rose's bed.

"Oh, of course! They would love to stick their needles in me and sell me their potions and make me feel worse in order to save me." She stopped speaking with a hiccup, and sat staring at her hands.

Rose looked up and studied Natalie's crestfallen face. "I know this is hard for everyone, but I am the one leaving." Natalie nodded, trying to understand how Rose must be feeling.

"And don't you worry about Felix. I will talk to him." Rose says this as if it is a royal declaration. As if it will fix everything between them.

"He is angry because I knew you were sick, and didn't tell him.

"I asked you not to tell anyone."

"Yes, but…"

"But what, Dear?"

"I am going to look so stupid… I didn't realize he was your son."

Rose chuckled and then coughed. As soon as she could breathe, she began to laugh again, which made her cough again. "Oh, Dear Natalie."

Natalie felt her cheeks heat. Looking back, she saw there were signs. Rose was so proud of Felix new apartment. Now, Natalie knew it was because he'd just moved out of her house. The fact that the staff all deferred to him if Rose wasn't reigning over the kingdom of Trailside. Natalie was focusing on other things and missed it all. And now she has ruined the best thing since… forever.

Rose interrupted her thoughts with a yawn. "I will talk to him, Dear Girl. Just, be sure about what you want so you don't hurt my boy. He's going to need someone special. I need to rest for a while now. Thank you for this visit." Her words were soft and plain-spoken.

Natalie leaned over the old woman and

hugged her gently, as if she was made of crystal. Rose caressed Natalie's cheek again, tears sparkling in her dark eyes.

CHAPTER 23

Girl's Night

Natalie inhaled deeply, enjoying the fragrant candles and the larger space of the living room. Her velvet couches and fuzzy blankets were tossed casually to look inviting and unfussy. She'd need someone to come hang the artwork that had started to arrive. She finally had begun to enjoy feathering this nest.

At last, she was free to soak in the ginormous house bought with her own money. She'd moved anything she cared about out of the pool house over here in the past few days. After Natalie came clean with Maisie and told her the full story, Maisie was gung ho to check out the big house. Maisie and Jessica had come over to help today, but they spent most of their time gawking at the six bedrooms and grand halls of the big house.

"It needs a name, it is so big." Maisie had chortled as she skated the halls in her socks. "Something like Nat's Castle, or The Bridgerton Estate." Maisie felt closer to Natalie after they shared their life stories weeks ago.

"You hate that show." Jessica's tone was

164

accusing but playful.

Maisie shrugged, "Dude, our pal is a Duchess, the house needs a big name."

"Halton House? That is where they filmed it, you know?" Jessica offered with a smile.

"Footsie Palace?" Maisie plunged her slim body down into a faux fur blanket on the loveseat as she crooned the name with a grin. Natalie's cheeks tinged pink with embarrassment. Jessica didn't yet know how Natalie had paid for this 'grand estate'. Maisie caught on quickly and changed the subject.

Natalie knew the big house was probably larger than anything these two girls had lived in, but she was proud of her accomplishments and enjoyed sharing them.

"How about 'The Castle'?" She suggested. Both girls nodded approval.

The house on Greenridge Circle, now named The Castle, was going to be a great place for her new life. When Natalie told her story to Maisie, easier now that she wasn't a murderess, she was surprised at how tightly Maisie hugged her. This pink-haired woman wasn't one for PDA, but her eyes shone with tears as she hugged Natalie fiercely and swore to support her through anything. Maisie told Natalie her own harrowing tale, and Natalie had yet to fully process her friend's painful story.

Eventually, the three of them congregated in the living room with big glasses of wine and the mood turned serious. Rose had left the hospital four days earlier, supposedly to recover at home. Word spread quickly through the TITS chat and everyone knew she was not actually going to recover. Grieving had begun. As her friends chattered in the background, Natalie's mind drifted.

Felix kept the plates spinning at Trailside, but he was often absent, tending to Rose at her home. Hospice was called, as was Scotty the coffee barista who had access to great strains of 'mary jane' as Rose had taken to calling it. Periodic puffs were the only way Rose could develop an appetite, and Scotty gave it away to the old girl for free now.

Felix still hadn't spoken to Natalie, other than to exchange updates with all staff about his mother, or to share work related details. She had texted and called him a few times, but knew she couldn't push it. The poor guy was losing his mother. Why would he care about her now? The whole restaurant team worked hard to serve delicious meals and keep both Rose and Felix from needing to worry about Trailside.

***

A party was planned for the next day at the restaurant. A mid-afternoon soiree, with Rose as the honored guest. Regulars to Trailside were casually notified, friends and family of the McCalls got phone calls or emails with the details. In Rose's words, it was a Soiree to Life, but they all knew it would be a goodbye party to the grand dame. At least they could do it while she was still living.

Plans were made, menus decided, and extravagant decor fit for a coronation felt futilely hopeful. Rose was adored and respected in Valparaiso, so the guest list would be standing-room only. The chef planned piles of appetizers and Jessica placed an order for extra cases of champagne.

Maisie and Natalie both went to see Rose every day. Natalie thought the beautiful lady was disappearing before her eyes, and it was heartbreaking. As Jessica and Maisie chattered about details for the party, Natalie's thoughts drifted to earlier that morning when she saw Rose. Felix couldn't leave fast enough when she arrived. He mumbled something about getting a shower at home and slipped out the door while Rose snored softly in her bedroom.

Natalie sunk silently into a green brocade armchair so as not to awaken Rose. She had a red wig on today, and it was either weirdly asymmetrical or had gone cockeyed as she slept. As long as Rose didn't know, it didn't matter. Even in these twilight days, she sported a strong lip color and whatever wig of the day she desired. She had dozens of them hanging on special forms on the walls of her bedroom. A rainbow of possibilities for a woman of many faces.

The group updates shared that Rose was supposed to be on oxygen, but she hated the contraption and rarely used it. It was getting hard to talk with her as she struggled to breathe. Natalie was content to scroll on her phone as Rose dozed.

"Nat-ta-lieee." She looked up, grinning at how Rose always pronounced every syllable of her name as if it was important all on its own. She pocketed her phone and joined Rose in bed, snuggling into the woman's paper embrace. The bedroom didn't smell medicinal, but perfumed, and Natalie appreciated the luxury evident in the room.

"Can I do anything for you?" She always asked, and Rose always said no.

"Yes." Natalie raised her eyebrows and waited for Rose to continue. "I want you to look into my jewelry box." Natalie moved to the large standing armoire that held her endless rainbow of jewelry. "No, not that one…the small blue one." Natalie looked for another box and spied it on Rose's dresser.

"What do you want to wear today?"

"What do you like best?"

Natalie looked over the sparkling jewelry and spied a lovely heart-shaped ruby ring. It was outlined in thick gold with a raised diamond and ruby center, it looked perfect for Rose. She brought it to the woman in her bed. "This is a gorgeous start!" She moved to slide it onto Rose's finger, but the woman curled Natalie's fingers around the ring instead.

"You keep it. You wear it." Natalie's mouth

dropped open, and she tried to protest. "You wanna…" Rose coughed feebly and swiped at her mouth, "…argue with a dying lady?" Natalie closed her mout,h and her objections died in her throat. She slipped the ruby ring onto her finger and showed Rose the ring with a smile.

"Thank you, Rose. It is lovely."

Rose had already dozed back off. Natalie wondered if she really could keep the ring, and decided Felix actually might speak with her about this.

The blonde shook her head, shifting from the past to the present. She looked at the ring on her hand, sitting in her house, on her velvet couch. Natalie's attention came back to her friends, and the party chatter. Her wine glass was empty.

"Girls, should I open another bottle? You both could stay; I have guest rooms made up for you already!"

Jessica and Maisie both shook their heads. Her friends made their apologies as they rose to head to their own homes. Tomorrow was the Soiree, and everyone would be up early to decorate. The restaurant would be closed until the party began.

CHAPTER 24

After You Get What You Want, You Don't Want It

Felix was frustrated with his mother. He'd unfolded the wheelchair, covered it in a velvet throw she kept in the back of her Cadillac 'just in case' and rolled the chair to her passenger door. She refused to get into the chair. Instead, she was attempting to pull herself up to standing and almost collapsed into his arms in a heap. She swayed as she held onto the door of the car and he held onto her.

"I will not roll into my party like an old lady. I will go in on your arm or not at all." The last words were faint as she struggled to breathe, struggling to live.

"Okay. How 'bout we roll to the door, then you walk in? How does that sound? You need to keep your strength up for your admirers; I don't think you will last long here."

She swatted him lightly, lacking the strength to impact him at all. "I will expire on my own timeline. I'm going to enjoy this soiree!" She sank gratefully into the hateful wheelchair, and Felix maneuvered her to the front door, as promised. Tom had been on the lookout for her arrival, as he stepped out just in time to take her other arm. The two men carried the weight of her in as if she merely floated between them.

"Thank you, Handsome, thank you too, Felix. I deeply appreciate such attractive escorts."

"Keep up that talk, and I will want you all to myself, Miss Rose." Tom teased as they eased her onto the upholstered chair placed in the middle of everything.

Rose sat in the chair as if it was a throne. She'd selected a black, sharply shaped wig for the occasion. It made her feel like Cleopatra, but the younger folks would think of Uma Thurman in the Pulp Fiction movie. She had a red lip and a rainbow of jewelry that looked too heavy for her frail body.

The music, food, and libations were all designed to emulate class and sophistication. The guests milled about, almost apologetic that they were enjoying the party. Everyone got small visits with Rose, talking about her beauty, how she had impacted their life or work or both. There was the sudden appearance of a tissue box on the table next to her as many *tete-a-tetes* ended with one or both parties in tears.

Natalie sat with Rose, and Tom joined her on the adjacent couch. Tom had called her a few times and tried to talk to her when she was working. Natalie had no interest in him anymore. She'd fallen for the nice guy. She wanted Felix.

When Tom became flirty with Natalie, Rose placed her hand in front of his rugged face dismissively. "That is quite enough Romeo, she is taken!"

Natalie began to splutter an objection when Maisie joined them, saying, "That is Thor, Rose."

Tom stood up, kissed Rose's hand and said, "Actually, Madame, my name is Tom." The three women laughed and he sauntered off. They couldn't help but watch him go.

"He is dumb, but damn, isn't he beautiful?" Maisie said, and Rose and Natalie murmured in agreement. Rose had a fit of coughing...so weak and flimsy it made Natalie miss her robust coughing episodes from a mere few weeks ago.

"Natalie, I think you have someone with whom you still need to converse." Rose gestured slightly with her jeweled hand, and Natalie saw Felix standing at the back of the dining room, watching them. She kissed Rose's cheek and nodded before leaving her side.

Natalie swiped two champagne flutes from a tray and made a beeline to Felix. To her surprise and tremulous delight, he stayed put, eyeing her as she approached.

"Fizz?" She asked, handing him one of the glasses. He took it, and swigged heavily from it before turning to face her. Anything she might have said clung to her dry throat. They just looked at each other for a few moments without speaking.

"Thank you, Natalie." He dropped his gaze to her mouth, and she allowed herself a slight smile. This was progress, right? He wasn't walking away. Natalie wanted to ask him why he refused all of her calls and texts, but that would put him on the defensive. If Rose had talked to him, maybe there was hope for them after all. He hadn't run away. He was being attentive, and he accepted the drink she offered. She wished the correct words would come to her.

She was so good at people, flirting, speaking, all of it... but her brain was tired. So much had happened in such a short time, and she was mentally and physically exhausted. Her game was gone when it came to this man.

"I have missed you." She said quietly, and thought he looked surprised at her words. He hid his face with the glass again, draining it.

"Oh? Thanks. I've been busy."

She set her full glass down on a ledge and hugged herself. She wore a clingy red top and black dress pants. She'd wanted to look classy and professional for the party, even if she wasn't working. Her blonde hair was in an updo to show off the sparky red earrings she'd chosen to complement her ruby ring from Rose. Tendrils had come loose with all the hugging from the party, and she blew them away from her face with an anxious huff.

"Of course. I know. I just meant..." *What did she mean? Ugh.* She felt eyes on her, and turned to see Rose's dark, watchful eyes on her. Encouraged, she tried again. "Felix, you are a nice guy–"

"Oh boy. Golly Ms. Zidler, just what every guy wants to hear!" He stepped back, looking irritated. Natalie closed the distance between them. Felix froze.

"Look, I don't trust people easily, and I trusted you."

He didn't say anything, just studied the wall, the empty glass in his hand. This wasn't going well.

"Felix, would you please date me?" Her voice was low and quiet, devoid of artifice. She stood facing him, resigned to accept any answer to her question.

He met her eyes, surprised and there was something else she couldn't name. "What?"

"Ugh! Felix, will you go on a date with me? Will you date me? I like you. I like who I am with you. I miss you."

He didn't say anything but started smiling and then touched her arm. The hand that held his glass was slack at his side, dregs of champagne dripping to the floor. "Really?"

"Yes. Yes. Didn't all that kissing tell you something?"

"Um, you had a big emotional dump; I thought maybe…"

"I like you, Felix. The past few weeks without talking to you have been terrible. You wouldn't return my calls or texts."

He pulled her into his chest, his glass joining hers on the ledge behind them. His voice was low, catching in his throat as he replied, "My mom is dying."

"I know. Felix, I am so sorry."

"My mom is dying, and you kept it from me." His voice was thick, and he squeezed her like a python. Natalie began to cry quietly into his warm shoulder as he held her. Her tears seeped out onto his black button-up shirt and she sniffled, bringing his good, earthy scent into her nose. "She said that should make me see you as trustworthy. You kept her secret."

Her reply was muffled, her mouth against his chest. "And?"

"I trust you, too, Natalie. You didn't realize, I guess, she was my mom. You just were being yourself. You are a kind, generous, sexy and yes, trustworthy, woman. I missed you, too. I worried about you when I could. We didn't get to finish talking, really."

She lifted her face to his before he could embarrass them both. She caught his mouth with hers and they kissed like the last two people on Earth. They picked right up where they left off. Mouths hungrily consumed each other, arms entwined, and she heard herself laugh against his mouth in relief. They pulled back to look at each other and she saw the damn fool was crying! That wasn't manly; that should be a turn off. Instead, her heart opened up to Felix like a magician's bouquet: with a snap and rainbow flourish of overwhelming beauty and goodness. She pulled him down to kiss her more, and they swayed together, oblivious to the world.

It wasn't until Natalie realized the pattering noise was applause that they extricated themselves from the kiss to look around them. The party guests were clapping and catcalling the lovers, and Felix blushed a deep red. His hands in her hair had rumpled the updo. Natalie lifted her fingers to the back of her hair to unpin it and shake it down around her shoulders. Felix smoothed a tendril of her hair and then held her by the hand. They both smiled sheepishly at their friends and tried to recover from the passionate embrace moments earlier.

Natalie's green eyes swept the crowd to find Rose. Maisie was still with her, grinning and swiping her pink hair to hide tears. The dying woman met Natalie's eyes as she slowly dropped two fingers from her lips, finished with the wolf whistle that had pierced the applause. This set off another round of razzing the young couple. The two women smiled at each other through the crowd, knowing life and death could both be good now.

CHAPTER 25

Let's Make Love

"Okay, so I have a weird question for you, Felix." Natalie and Felix sat on the counter in Rose's black granite kitchen. They had been sorting unnecessary things as she slept. In one of the many conversations Felix did not want to have with his mother, she'd encouraged him to sell her home and buy a new house for himself. Sorting belongings now kept Rose in the loop, when she was awake. It also gave them something to do when she slept.

"No pressure…" She laughed, and he stopped breathing for a moment, just to extend the sensation of her joy.

"Can I see your bookshelves?" She looked mischievous, waiting for his reply.

"What? Here? I moved all my things to the apartment."

"Yes I know, I mean at your apartment."

He cocked an eyebrow at her, setting the pan he held into the waiting mover's box. It felt weird and wrong to pack up his mother's belongings while she was alive. She'd chided them all into looting her home, packing up and giving away junk and a myriad of tasks to make the end easier on all of them, particularly Felix. Natalie was always there to help him, and he knew he was falling hard for this generous, gorgeous woman. They had not taken the relationship further; his mother and their jobs took all the energy they had. He was sure the woman beside him couldn't be suggesting an afternoon delight? He figured a joke would suffice.

"Well, that is a weird way to try to sleep with me, Sweetling."

Natalie rolled her eyes and scoffed at him. He wasn't sure if it was his joke or that wretched, accidental endearment. "I'm never sleeping with you if I don't like your nightstand."

He grew still and stood to face her. "I...I have condoms."

Natalie looked confused but stopped swinging her legs. "What?"

"In the nightstand. But I'm not quite –".

Her whisper was shrill in the quiet house. "Not that, you Doofus! Books. I want to see if you have books on your nightstand."

Felix looked perturbed and leaned against the counter. "Of course, I have books. Who doesn't?"

Natalie's lips quirked and she replied, "Lots of people, guys especially."

"You are judging them, aren't you?"

She giggled and tossed her shiny blonde

hair. "Absolutely. But, I have high hopes for you, after the Chaucer quote."

Felix racked his brain to pick up what she was laying down. He drew a blank.

"Sleeping dogs." She waited, stroking his arm as her legs swung again from her seat on the counter.

"Oh right!" He laughed. "Of course, peruse away. Do you have a time in mind?" They were either working, staying with Rose, or sleeping at their respective places; too tired for anything romantic. Felix thought, despite everything, that he might be up for something more.

Natalie pursed her lips and thoughtfully tapped her chin. "I dunno. Are you busy right now?"

Felix almost dropped the dish he held and deftly slipped it into the top of the box he was filling.

"A sweet guy in a black t-shirt really gets me going." His mouth went dry, and his heart tugged.

Natalie pulled out her cell phone and tapped away while he struggled to remember words. He was usually good at words. Why did he feel so dumb around this blonde?

"I don't feel right leaving–" She showed him the phone screen and the text she'd received. Maisie was ten minutes away, ready for her turn to keep the sleeping Rose company. "Well, alrighty then," he finished.

Felix gulped, and Natalie giggled as she

pulled him to her against the counter for a long, slow kiss. They had both been overwhelmed and exhausted the past week, but right now, he felt so energized he could run all the way home. He could do anything if Natalie was with him.

***

"I thought you wanted to look at my books?" The blonde before him had teased him on the entire drive to his apartment. Now that they were inside his door, she had not taken her lips off of his as they fumbled towards his bedroom. It seemed he wasn't the only one with a strange blast of energy because of their attraction.

"Oh, I do want to look at your books. There's some other things I'm more interested in right now." He felt himself tighten, swell and throb against the zipper of his jeans. Could he be even bigger because of her interest in him? Was he smarter and more attractive because Natalie Zidler was in his arms? Felix thought he'd never been so hard in his entire life. *Will I be man enough for her?* he wondered. *Or, am I going to blow this in the first ten seconds?*

Oh my God, if I cum in my pants, she'll never speak to me again. But even these nervous thoughts could not stick around with Natalie's mouth on his.

"I have condoms," he said, and she nodded against him. She was biting his neck and shoulders rougher than he expected her to be. Her breasts pressed against his chest, not quite falling out of her bra, and he felt as if he was having an out-of-body experience. The two entwined lovers disregarded the disheveled condition of the apartment, landing together with a laugh and some awkward elbow moments on his queen-sized bed. Felix was thankful that making the bed every morning was a habit that he had found satisfying.

Natalie threw him on his back and straddled him, smiling at him and caressing his face with her hand. He could barely breathe, and she looked down between her legs at the bulge in his jeans appreciatively.

"I like the way you're thinking." He laughed, uncertain and so taken with the movement of her lips. *How is her lipstick still there?* It was like a nice pink with some kind of glitter, but there was nothing on her cheeks, only her beautifully shaped full lips. He would never understand women, especially not this one, but he sure as hell liked them.

"What do you want? You are in charge..." His voice was a mere whisper. She shook her head and said,

"No. No, we are in charge. This is for both of us, isn't it?" She rolled to the side of him to lay against his body. He traced her features with his fingertips, making her shiver. Felix dropped his fingers down the side of her neck and along her collarbone and shoulder. Natalie was wearing one of those dresses she often wore that stopped just

HEATHER CURLEE NOVAK

above her knees. He cautiously ran his hand along her hip and slid the dress up against her middle, exposing her thigh and sexy purple underpants.

"This is for both of us, then; I can get with that. We've had a hell of a time getting here." They embraced as friends rather than lovers for a moment until their nearness turned both of them towards carnality.

They kissed and bit each other's lips, and the heat between their bodies sparked and grew. Felix let his hands run wherever they'd wanted to be ever since he met this woman. He wandered and explored her body freely until finally, she helped him remove her sundress, leaving her in a purple lace bra and purple panties. His breath stopped in his throat and he just grinned at her as if he were a thirteen-year-old boy looking at a woman for the first time.

"You look like a young boy seeing a woman for the first time, and I like it." Her voice purred over his skin until the next part. "Felix, I'm not your first, am I?"

He blushed mightily, shaking his head 'No'. His words caught once again in his throat. Why did she do this to him so much? Sure, he adored her, loved her, and wanted her.

He what? You what? Fuck that man. Don't you say a word. Oh my God, you're going to blow it, dude. The voice inside his head was loud.

The whole time he argued with himself in his head, she lay beside him roving his body with

182

her soft hands. Then she let him explore her body with his eyes and his mouth and his warm, warm, warm hands. He slipped his hands inside her bra to cup her breasts, running his thumb over the pebbled nipples and dropping his mouth to them to slide his tongue over them. He wanted to bite them, but he didn't know what she liked yet, so he resisted.

She pressed herself against him, and his cock ached so badly he had to get his pants off. It was as if she could read his mind. He felt her hands at the button and zipper of the jeans, and pretty soon, he was in his boxers. She reached out and held him in her hands– both hands– he was pleased to see. He felt like the sexiest, coolest man on the face of the earth.

He almost told her he loved her then, but he bit his tongue to keep it inside. He didn't want to frighten this woman away. They had grown so close recently, but they didn't have the time to develop a relationship that would really weave them together like he wanted. Natalie was touching him inside his underpants, had slid them down at some point, and her mouth was on him, and he just about lost his fucking mind right then and there. She moaned and slid her mouth up and down over him. He would swear the bed tilted and spun in the room.

He had never experienced anything like this in his entire life. While he ached to experience her fully, he didn't think he was gonna last. He certainly hoped that wasn't a deal breaker. Felix knew he should probably pull her mouth away from him so that he could do something for her, but he could not. He was weak with desire. And then, and then, and then, and then: He orgasmed, plummeting over the cliff of love and desire for this woman.

He looked down just in time to see her take his cum into her mouth, and he died right then and there. She pulled back to wipe her mouth, grinning at him as if he had done her a favor. Natalie lay against him afterward, murmuring something in his ear that he couldn't even understand. It was as if the English language was never his to begin with. As if she murmured some magical incantation in another language. But then, after a moment, his brain showed back up, thank God, and told him he'd better do the same for her.

Felix pulled Natalie to him, kneeling over her. "I'm sorry. I'm so sorry."

She laughed and said lightly, "Did you not think I knew what I was doing? This isn't my first time, darling, but it certainly matters more than before."

He heard her, but he couldn't talk to her at that moment. He slid her dark purple underpants down over her full hips and thighs. Running his hand down the pebbly sides of her thighs where cellulite hid under her skirts. He squeezed these big thighs, these full, textured goddess thighs, and parted them gently so that he could see her.

He sucked in a breath and could have looked at her for an hour. It was like nothing he had ever seen before. She looked like a piece of art, like Georgia O'Keeffe's flowers. She looked like an aurora borealis. Natalie's vagina opened to him like some kind of portal. He felt himself get hard again, which was absolutely insane.

He was in charge now. Felix lowered his mouth to her entrance, licking tentatively and tasting her saltiness. He leaned in with his tongue to find the top hood part and the button that he had read about. The clitoris, the part that should bring her all the things she had just brought to him. She gasped slightly and put her hands in his hair, guiding him a little higher to just the right place.

"Deeper," she said. "More." She moaned as he got more comfortable kissing this part of her. Her pubic hair tickled his nose and face, and he drank in the musky scent of her, which flooded his senses. It combined with whatever perfume she wore. His hands gripped her thighs, digging into them as he spread her wider, and kissed her further and deeper.

Soon, she was moaning, and he thought he could just die right now and be so happy, but he still had more work to do. He continued doing the alphabet and kissing her pussy like a mouth and all the things he had read to prepare for this moment. Soon, she was touching herself and bucking underneath his mouth, and she was wetter than before, and she was calling his name.

After her orgasm, she lay loose and flushed against him, panting and smiling like she was drunk. He could hardly believe she was here, and she was his.

And then he was hard, aching, and in need of her once again.

CHAPTER 26

Life is a Cabaret

The beloved great lady, Rose McCall, expired later that week. It was a Tuesday afternoon, and the weather had just turned cool. Leaves began to turn colors in some places, and candles scented with cinnamon set a cozy mood in the sad house. Rose lounged in her bed like a queen, dozing while Felix read "The Light We Carry," by Michelle Obama, in the next room. He'd just noted the quote in his journal:

"I lean on each individual
at different times
and in different ways."

The passage made him think of his friends, his mother's friends, and how everyone surrounded them as Rose's health quietly failed. He yawned and looked at the clock to see it was almost five o'clock. Natalie and Maisie were due any moment with tacos for dinner. He stretched and stood to check on his mother. As he walked down the hall, unbeknownst to her only child,

Rose took a thin breath in, let it out, and drifted away.

Felix knew something changed in the dim stillness of the room.

"Mom?" He spoke out of habit. She hadn't spoken in several days. Hospice was there off and on to help out and administer the 'joy juice' as she'd called it when she still spoke. Her breathing was so shallow that her not breathing made no difference. When he sat down beside her on the bed, Felix reached for her hand but already knew she had made her final exit.

Rose's face looked so relaxed, and she was still under the tousled auburn wig Maisie had put on her as she slept the day before. His mother's hand, still warm in his, didn't shift or flex as he held it.

He didn't cry. He only felt relief that she left on her terms, in her home, in her bed. Not every person would have this last luxury.

Eventually, the girls came, calling jovially down the hallway until they came to Rose's door and understood. Natalie kneeled beside the bed, her arms around his waist as he held his dead mother's hand. Maisie eased up to the head of the bed, and leaned over to straighten Rose's bangs gently. She kissed her own fingertips and placed them against the old woman's cheek before backing out of the room. Maisie's voice carried to them as she called the hospice nurse and then Trailside, to let them know.

The tacos lay forgotten in their jaunty plastic carrier bag as the living cared for the dead.

***

Natalie sat beside Felix through the memorial service for Rose McCall. The decision was unspoken. It just happened, and they were both grateful to be together. Natalie charmed all of Felix's extended family as they arrived in Valparaiso in the days before the service. Natalie was officially introduced as his girlfriend, but Maisie rarely missed a moment between the two girls to purr about engagement ring options in Rose's vast jewelry collection.

"Stop it! That is inappropriate, Maisie!" Natalie felt safe with Felix, but it had only been a month or so since everything happened, and she was still reeling from the extraordinary changes. "I'm not interested in getting married, no matter what you and Rose think!" Maisie just chuckled behind her hand, and moved on to the next guest there to pay their respects to the great Rose McCall.

Right up until the end, Rose had gently encouraged Natalie to be serious about Felix for the long haul. During one of their last visits, barely one week ago, her scratchy voice implored, "will you marry my boy, Natalie?"

Not wanting to disappoint a dying woman, she'd replied, "I am falling in love with your son, but we have a lot of time to spend together before discussing marriage, Rose."

The older woman spoke softly to the beautiful blonde with her. "He has always been so smart and so quiet. Don't break his heart." Rose drifted off then, but Natalie stayed beside her, smoothing the down comforter over the tiny woman.

She spoke quiet, private words only meant for her older friend. "I won't. I hope he doesn't decide I am too much for him. I am afraid he might just be smart enough not to want me, once he really knows me. When the shine is off of whatever this is. I like him so very much, and he makes me feel so safe and valuable despite my flaws. You raised a good man, Rose. He is a good man."

Natalie was startled when Rose spoke almost imperceptibly. "My son is going to marry you. I am disappointed– " Rose sighed, offered a thin rattling cough, and finished, "I won't be there to dance at your wedding." Natalie's ear barely heard the whispered words, but her heart received them loud and clear as her eyes filled with tears.

***

Three weeks later, Natalie lay wrapped up in a quilt beside the pool. The chilly air couldn't keep her from being outside when the sun was shining so warmly. She let her mind wander over the weeks and then months since Rose's death. She and Felix had grown closer, and she felt more alive than ever before. She laughed quietly to herself when she realized the truth: She would say yes when Felix proposed.

While it might not be enough time for a rational person to commit, they loved each other already. The events of their lives set them on the fast track to emotional intimacy. She had witnessed how Felix handled hard things, and how deeply he could love other people. While she never thought a nice, normal guy would catch her eye, Natalie knew she wanted to be with Felix for the rest of her life. He made her feel safe, accepted her wildness, and was a kind person. And they were great in bed together.

It didn't hurt that among the stack of nonfiction offerings and random detective novels, he also had books like Sandra Cisneros' The House on Mango Street and The Jakarta Pandemic by Steve Konkoly. A varied bookshelf, good in bed, and kindness were the things that made Natalie's bombshell heart go pitter-pat. He'd even been lifting at the gym and running. She warmed at the thought of their earlier indoor activities and grinned. As she let her mind wander over his sexy body, his piercing eyes, his growing muscles, an idea flittered.

She had been the one to ask him out on a date after everything happened. Sure, Rose had instigated, but the old lady wasn't wrong. Maybe Natalie would be the one to propose, one of these days when the time was perfect. The blonde woman smiled to herself and twisted the ruby heart ring on her right hand as she daydreamed.

Natalie Zidler had future plans for a nice guy who loved her just as she was.

Dear Reader, Bombshell and Friend,

I am giddy you read this little Bombshell Beauties book of mine! I hope you enjoyed these characters and found a bit of yourself in the best of them.

As an author, reading and writing are my favorite ways to spend time, and none of us have enough of that precious currency. Thank you for spending some of yours with me.

Here is the first chapter of the next book in the "Bombshell Beauties" series. The working title is "Pink." You will recognize the main character right away. Her story is a doozy, and I hope you will stay friends with her long enough to see it through.

Love,

Heather

Bombshell Beauties Book 2
Sneak Peek: PINK

Part of the Story

The heavy knife slipped in her sweaty, bloody hands as she pointed it at the old woman. The wrinkled old battle axe panted, keeping her eyes on the knife and the young girl behind it. Her hands were spread in a supplication gesture, her greying hair loosening from a tight topknot. Blood was already on her blue silk suit as the two women circled each other warily.

Two men stood back, observing without interfering unless the old crone called for them. The girl holding the knife lunged, making contact with the woman's ample middle, but the knife slid out of her damp hands and clattered to the floor.

"Pick it up, Little One. You can do better." The old woman seemed to change her demeanor from opponent to teacher.

A new voice from behind them rang out, "Stop, Matilde. Please leave her out of this!"

The girl and the old woman ignored the blonde tied to a chair at the other end of the room. The warehouse was full of boxes, dripping pipes, and darkness. Five people were present, and only three would leave the building that night.

The pink-haired girl had tears rolling down her cheeks."I can't do it, Mama. I'm so sorry." She wiped her snotty nose on the back of her hand and stood with her arms limp, hopelessly waiting for the inevitable.

CHAPTER 1 Don't Mess with Pink

A petite girl with radiant pink hair wrestled an overloaded shopping cart with a wonky front wheel. No one noticed or cared as she shoved and maneuvered the cart out of the grocery store into the busy parking lot. Her tiny middle finger popped up as she smiled at the shiny black car that swerved past her instead of letting her cross. Maisie took things in stride, but not without retaliation.

She began unloading bags into the hatchback of a car too ancient to be easily recognized. It was a bright blue 1995 Ford Fiesta with too many miles to count. The girl had to hold the hatchback door up with one arm as she loaded groceries with the other. The trunk slammed shut, and she returned the cart to the cart rack.

Anyone watching could tell she was crafty, and would probably steal the dentures right out of your mouth without you minding all that much. The girl wore a floral shirt, clashing floral shorts above pale bare legs, and black boots. She had a sly look about her as if she couldn't be trusted, but if your eyes met hers, she radiated innocence and warmth. It was an intoxicating and maddening combination.

Lacing her keys between her pale knuckles, she approached her tired, old car. Maisie scraped the tip of a key against the shiny black car that had pulled in next to her Fiesta. A nails-on-chalkboard sound filled her ears as the key peeled paint and scraped an ugly scratch into the vehicle's side from the tail light to the passenger door. Maisie's heart beat faster as she cast a singular backward glance. No one had noticed what she did. Good.

Maisie Szabo looked much younger than she was. At twenty-five, she faced life head-on, getting kicked in the teeth more often than she cared to admit. Her current baggage consists of groceries, including ginger ale, saltines, and bleach wipes. She still lived at home with her father, who had the flu. She didn't mind looking after him and didn't have to go to work for several hours.

Maisie worked at a local Valparaiso restaurant called Trailside. The main staff, who had been there since they opened two and half years ago, called themselves The Independent Trailside Society, or TITS. She'd been pleased to find a server position at Trailside last year. The owner was a kooky older lady who wore lots of jewelry and a different wig daily. The owner's son, Felix, had asked Maisie out when she first started working there, but he was not her type, and she turned him down. He was a great friend, and they had loads of fun together at work.

The only problem was she still lived at home.

"Dad?" She whispered as she slipped in the back door with one of the grocery bags. If Jerry Szabo was sleeping, she wanted to let him be.

"In here. Glad you're back." Her dad's voice

sounded tired. He was not barfing today, but last night, she swore never to have kids if that was a hint of what it would be like. Gross.

Maisie unloaded one of the ginger ales and a sheath of Saltine crackers onto the coffee table next to his water and the empty puke bowl. The bowl also happened to be the most enormous Tupperware bowl they owned, and it usually held buttered popcorn for movie nights. Gross again.

"Did you have enough?" He asked quietly. His sandy brown hair looked greasy, and the lines around his face seemed deeper. When had her father gotten old?

"Yup."

"Thanks for going. I'm sorry about all of this."

Maisie snorted. "Whaddya mean? Like you never looked after me?"

Her dad shifted on the couch, reached for the crackers, and munched thoughtfully. "Yeah, I see your point."

"Uh, I gotta go to work in a bit. There is a can of chicken noodle if you are feelin' it later." She clicked her tongue, waiting for his reply.

"Okay." Jerry leaned back on the couch again, still holding half a cracker as his eyes closed and he drifted back to sleep.

***

Maisie Szabo and her dad had been together since her mom, Paulina, left when Maisie was twelve. She remembered like it was yesterday. She had not told anyone what happened, but it burned in her chest like a held breath; it wanted out. Even all these years later, her eyes burned, remembering the hurt and pain of her mother being there one moment and gone the next.

It wasn't like they had a good mother-daughter relationship. Paulina was a singular kind of woman with high expectations for everyone around her, including herself. Maisie remembered hours under the hairbrush as her mother would brush out her thick, long blonde hair, complementing it and chiding Maisie to take better care of herself. Maisie barely got a chance to care for her hair because her mother took it over from the day she was born. Every day, she was tricked out in braids, updos, or whatever the heck Paulina thought looked beautiful.

Her mother instilled in her the importance of taking care of oneself. And of appearance opening or closing doors. Success in life, according to her mother, was determined solely by whether you had brushed your hair or not.

Her mother dressed her in floral dresses and old lady pantyhose with slippery shoes that felt uncomfortable on the school playground. Maisie felt overdressed at school, but when she complained to her mother, her mother reminded her again that what opened doors was one's appearance. Paulina's Golden Rule was a woman should always look her best, comfort be damned. *Beauty before comfort* rang in Maisie's ears long after Paulina disappeared.

Maisie loved her mother, and like most daughters with a demanding mother, she worked hard to earn her approval. Pauline's approval was fleeting and hard to find. She was self-absorbed and interested only in living the good life. Maisie thought they lived a good life, but her mother often harassed her father about expectations, and she heard their sharp voices late at night when she was supposed to be asleep.

Her mother would say, "This isn't what I signed up for!" Maisie could imagine how she would toss her thick, frosted blonde bob as she spoke.

Her father would say, "Paulina, I love you."

Her mother would screech, "You can do better. Why aren't you asking for that Manager position?"

Her father would say, "Paulina, Beloved, I love you. Isn't that enough?"

The fights never lasted long, but the silence between her parents was endless.

The house always looked immaculate, and her mother bought things that her father would complain about being too expensive. The house on Center Street in Valparaiso was small, with three tiny bedrooms, one bathroom, a smaller living room, and an eat-in kitchen. Paulina would throw soft blankets over the shabby furniture and often drooled over the houseware displays in stores at prices even she knew were out of reach. Maisie's father, Jerry, would plant seeds in old pots and water them carefully. The pots would slowly reveal beautiful flowers, and he would place them on the front porch steps. They made their shabby little house look almost pretty. Even Paulina would stop to admire the look of them on the steps.

They weren't a happy family, but Maisie found snatches of happiness when she could. The way her mother looked at her father when the three of them sat on the porch was one of her favorite memories. Her father recited haiku poetry to them at the dinner table, which was another. Jerry would ask, "May I regale you ladies with some fine words I wrote today?" Maisie would roll her eyes, but when Jerry spouted prose, Paulina seemed to unfold from herself. She would take his hand, and her eyes would glisten with emotion. Maisie could imagine them as in love then, but it was fleeting.

Once her mother left, it was just Maisie and her dad. It felt like some glow had left the house, though it was quieter and more peaceful. Macy did her best to care for her dad after her mom left. She would make him eggs and burnt toast in the morning. She would try to pack lunches if there was lunch meat and bread and mayonnaise. In the thirteen years they lived together without Paulina, her father had never brought another woman home. All of the life seemed to have left him without his wife around.

Maisie did her homework at the kitchen table and sometimes put in a Stouffer's lasagna so dinner could be ready when her father got home. Sometimes, she forgot to take the cardboard off the top of the package; it would be smoking and burned when he got in the house. They couldn't afford to order pizza, so they ate the charcoal mess with false cheer.

Maisie had to remind her father about her birthday, and when his birthday rolled around, she would either make him a card on computer printer paper or buy a dollar store card if she had a few bucks. They didn't celebrate her mother's birthday. Jerry had wanted to, and Maisie would be furious, biting back tears before storming off and slamming the door of her room. If Jerry Szabo honored his departed wife in any manner, it was private and not something Maisie had to endure.

ABOUT THE AUTHOR

Heather Curlee Novak

Heather Curlee Novak, AKA the 'Lazy Bombshell,' writes spicy suspense stories packed with humor, unexpected twists, and unforgettable characters who feel like lifelong friends. She's a lover of all things sparkly, cheeky, and mischievous—qualities that shine through in her work.

When she's not crafting tales of intrigue and laughter, Heather enjoys motivational speaking and draws inspiration from her years in customer service, sales training, and troubleshooting. Her professional experience fuels her ability to weave relatable, dynamic stories that resonate with readers.

Happily married to her real-life Prince Charming, John, Heather cherishes time with their two fascinating daughters, whom they encourage to live boldly and authentically. She lives each day passionately, striving to "live her love out loud" and bring joy, humor, and a touch of spice to everything she does.

BOOKS BY THIS AUTHOR

Small Man, Big Murder: Truth Is Easier To Fabricate Than Fiction. (Elm Street Stories Book 1)

Small Man, Big Murder is a short and spicy revenge story mostly invented by a feral middle-aged housewife. Follow Chad and his girlfriend Tiffany as they try to make money for the lifestyle they both desperately want. Meet the Bacon Babes and see how this tight-knit group of women ensures Chad gets what he deserves most. This is a love story, a hate story, and above all an idiot's guide to getting away with murder.

A Little Bitter

A Little Bitter is an adventurous romp through the sleepy Indiana town where Lola Messer was murdered in Small Man, Big Murder. Invented by a bored, middle-aged housewife lounging in silky bathrobes, we follow a woman scorned as she tries to make sense of her destroyed life. She's out to get revenge for herself and everyone who is a little bitter.

Roxy Babbit sacrificed her feisty soul for mundane marriage and motherhood, only to find herself adrift eighteen years later in a midlife crisis with no joy, style, or husband.

Will her 'Little Bitter' revenge business pave the way to financial stability, or create more catastrophes when she targets the town's famous but immoral Realtor?

A must-read if you, too, are A Little Bitter.

First & Last

In the wake of Lola Messer's gruesome murder, the tranquil town of Valpo is thrown into turmoil. The killer slips through the cracks of justice, leaving the community shattered and fear-stricken. For the Messer family, the trauma is compounded by the task of rebuilding their lives. As they grapple with their shattered world, two young sisters face an agonizing choice: remain in the shadow of the crime or escape to forge a new beginning elsewhere.
In this poignant conclusion to the Elm Street Story series, journey with the Messer family as they navigate their path to healing, uncover

new love, and confront the enduring bonds of family and resilience. Will the echoes of the past haunt their every step, or will they find strength in the promise of a fresh start? Discover the transformative power of hope and the indelible power of blood in this gripping finale.

Cat Dish Gin

Is this all there is in life?
An easy path towards being a better human!
LAUGH
CRY
DO SOMETHING
DIFFERENT
Cat Dish Gin: Have more fun in life, sex, parenting, and aging through self-care quickies!